DUPLICITY

IN 3 ACTS

DUPLICITY IN 3 ACTS

An Inspector Willis murder mystery by

Ray Klausen

ISBN: 978-1-961869-03-5

Cover design by David Pina

Cover photograph by Inarik, licensed by Adobe Stock

Interior design: Thomas Edward West of Amarna Books & Media.

First print edition 2023

Amarna Books & Media
Philadelphia, PA
www.amarnabooksandmedia.com

Dedication

To H.R. Nicholson, the best partner

and friend one could ask for.

Acknowledgements

I wish to acknowledge the following people for their help and support in making this book a reality:

Chris Cohen
Naomi Gerbarg
Rosemary Harris
Dana Ivey
Jeff Lee
Philip MacKethan
Rebecca Sawyer-Fay
Carol Smith
Barbara Wernick
Thomas Edward West
David Zippel

Table of Contents

Prologue..1

Act One, Scene 1..5
Act One, Scene 2..19
Act One, Scene 3..21
Act One, Scene 4..31
Act One, Scene 5..43
Act One, Scene 6..63

Act Two, Scene 1..69
Act Two, Scene 2..79
Act Two, Scene 3..103
Act Two, Scene 4..117

Act Three, Scene 1...133
Act Three, Scene 2...139
Act Three, Scene 3...149
Act Three, Scene 4...165
Act Three, Scene 5...175

Epilogue...189

Duplicity:

deceitfulness or double-dealing

Recipe for death:

Take an out-of-control ego with a celebrated
indifference toward others and mix in a
person with an obsession for revenge.
Yield: one murder.

Harold Gibson and **Trish Gibson**

In association with Lilah Townsend and Harry Carlone

Present

Dawna   Clarrisa
DRAKE   ROMAN

in

MAD ABOUT THE GAL!

Inspired by *Waiting in the Wings* by Noel Coward

Book by	Music by	New Lyrics by
Lefteris and Blom	Noel Coward et al.	Lenny Leith

with

Cora Williams	Romain Rodgers	Sally White

and

Marshall Ward

Sets by	Costumes by	Lighting by
Jens	Elina Fay	Fiona Nicholson

Musical Director	Stage Manager	Choreography by
Tad Morley	Peggy Rand	Kevin Travis

Wardrobe Supervisor	Prop Master	Fight Captain
Roz Hanson	Tony Krasne	Felix Ruddner

Directed by

Allison Duprey

Special appearance by

The 3 in 1 Investigation Agency

Inspector Willis	Ross Langley	Monty Anderson

and featuring

Natalie Reynolds	Carol Ward	Charma as herself

Prologue

Earlier, Dawna Drake, the star of the new Broadway-bound musical *Mad about the Gal*, had her driver bring her to the theatre, even though the Ritz Carlton, where she was ensconced, was just a few blocks from the Colonial Theatre. She certainly could use the exercise, since her dance numbers weren't very taxing; nevertheless, she never walked if she could be driven. And even if she wanted to walk, she always made it a point of keeping the public at a proper distance. After all, she was a star!

The show would be trying out in Boston for four weeks before it was to open on Broadway, just 10 weeks from now. Earlier, Dawna's limo (part of her lucrative contract with the show's producers) had pulled up to the stage door and Carl, her driver, quickly ran around to open the door for Dawna so she could sweep from the car to the stage door without making eye contact with the few fans who had patiently waited with their autograph books in hand.

Dawna greeted Harry, the stage doorman, with a warm, if somewhat put-on, smile (her standard "Hello, sorry, but I'm too important to stop" greeting) and swept past him to her star dressing room. She entered and did a quick survey to make sure that Nat, her assistant, dresser, and sometime confidante, had everything in place.

Especially important were her flowers, which were usually from her admirers but sometimes had to be augmented if the number had dwindled too much. She also made sure her mail had been sorted. She noted that the stack wasn't as large a usual and this really pissed her off. Also, she checked that her Perrier with a slice of lime and "just a splash of vodka" to fuel her vocal cords was sitting on her dressing table.

Also on her dressing room table was a unique arrangement of exotic green and purple orchids unlike any she had ever seen. "*Hmmmm*," she thought, "*I wonder who sent these?*"

Fingering the flowers, she realized with disgust that they were fake. She hated fake flowers! Dawna picked up the attached envelope, opened it, and took out the note that was printed and not handwritten in green ink.

THESE FLOWERS ARE LIKE YOU:
BEAUTIFUL BUT ARTIFICIAL AND FAKE.
ONE WONDERS IF THE WORLD WOULD
LIKE TO KNOW JUST HOW MUCH
YOU RESEMBLE THEM AND IF, LIKE
THESE FLOWERS, YOU'LL SOON BE
DESTROYED FOR BEING WHAT
YOU ARE… A FAKE, A FRAUD
AND MORE EVIL THAN ANYONE KNOWS!

In a fury, Dawna made a big scene of crumpling up the card and throwing the arrangement in the toilet, trying to flush it down and promptly clogging the works. She then proceeded to demand that her assistant Nat call the theatre manager and "Have him find a plumber to get that fucking toilet fixed and fixed DAMNED QUICK!"

Act 1, Scene 1
Putting on a Show

Harold Gibson, known by all as just "Gibson," was not a man to dwell in the past. What Gibson came up with was the idea of creating a new musical loosely based on—but totally different from—Noel Coward's play *Waiting in the Wings*, which had experienced a modicum of popularity in 1999 when Lauren Bacall and Rosemary Harris starred in a revival of the play on Broadway. What Gibson envisioned was a similar plot, reworked using a collection of Noel Coward's songs with a new scenario that would revolve around a group of performers who now lived in an actor's home. He, of course, felt it would "play" better if it were not an old-age retirement home. This way a top actress, a Lauren Bacall type, would agree to take on the starring role and not be stigmatized as being "old."

Often he would sit in his very neat and organized office and mull over the idea. The more he thought about it, the more he liked it. The test of time would be if he could sell it and make some much-needed money. His office was large, had a huge staff and, as it was in the middle of the theatre district, consequently cost a small fortune to run. His wife and producing partner, Trish, shared his concern.

Initially, his concept was met with lukewarm enthusiasm, but perseverance was Gibson's strong suit. He enlisted some well-established writers to rewrite the show's concept into what he thought was a fun, workable, and, more importantly, a bankable show. The time had now come to seriously move forward and in a moment of inspiration, Gibson had come up with the idea of casting Dawna Drake in the main role and Clarrisa Roman in the adversary role. Some might call it "typecasting," as Dawna and Clarrisa were less than friendly toward one another in real life, similar to the lead characters in the play.

While Clarrisa had many admirers in the theatre world and Dawna had in the past experienced considerable success in theatre, television, and film, neither actress had enjoyed anything that resembled a recent success. Gibson felt it possible to reach an agreement with the ladies in a fairly easy manner… that is, get their signatures on the dotted line. Once the ladies were on board, it would be easier to raise the capital for mounting the production. To add to the theatrics of the show, Gibson thought about casting Marshall Ward as Dawna's leading man. Ward was a handsome actor who at the time was, in fact, the leading man in Dawna's not-so-private life. As it turned out, he ended up not having a "long-term" contract. Nevertheless, it was just a matter of signing up the leading talent and, hopefully, the rest of the production would fall into place.

However, while landing Dawna as the star of the show would help tremendously in raising money to finance the show, he had created a huge problem for himself, in that normally a new show in development would have countless rehearsals and showcases to test out the show's material and maybe even go out of town to, say La Jolla or a place like the Denver Center where it would be far enough from prying eyes while they tested the material. But while Dawna's being connected to the show certainly helped the financial end of production, he now could end up with a fabulous cast and the needed money to put the show together but he would never get someone of Dawna's caliber to "workshop" the show, that is, fine tune the material. A difficult and dangerous situation. He could lose everything, and this show had to be a success for his production company to survive.

On a late summer morning that gave a hint of a premature Indian summer, Gibson called Dawna. "Good morning, Dawna, Gibson here. I hope I'm not calling you too early."

Gibson cheerfully said, hoping he would catch Dawna in a good and receptive mood. One never called a celebrity of Dawna's standing before 11:00 AM as ladies of her ilk tended to stay up late and needed their beauty rest. Consequently, they were not usually receptive to an early business call, but a call spiced up with a bit of gossip just might entice a receptive response from someone such as Dawna.

Gibson called with the express purpose of setting up a luncheon date with Dawna at Orso on West 46th Street, located just east of Joe Allen's, the famous show biz hangout. The restaurant had three advantages: it was quiet, glamorous, and was Dawna's favorite restaurant. And so, after some idle chitchat and gossip, it was arranged for Gibson to pick up Dawna the next day at 1:00 PM in his chauffeured, immaculate black limo that, despite the notorious filth of New York City, was always impeccably clean. The limo was his major means of transportation in the City and often served as a secondary office. Many a deal had been nailed in that car.

While Gibson normally would have had his secretary make the luncheon reservation, in this case he called the restaurant personally, discreetly found out which table Dawna favored, and made sure that her particular table would be held for this all-important luncheon. He also had a package delivered to the restaurant that was to be placed on one of the chairs at that table per his instructions.

Promptly at 1:00, Gibson arrived at Dawna's Fifth Avenue apartment building, left the car, and entered her apartment lobby, a festival of gleaming white marble with gold detailing. He asked the doorman to announce that Harold Gibson was "Here to pick up Miss Drake." After what appeared to be an unnecessary wait, the lobby elevator door opened to reveal Dawna Drake looking smashing in a totally impractical but highly theatrical all-white outfit: white suit, white Prada shoes and purse, and white fox fur, perhaps a bit out of style but pure "Dawna." Her "look" included her red hair which was highlighted with flecks of gold. Smashing… a dazzling image in that white marble lobby. Her gold jewelry picked up the room's gold accents. *"Hmmm,"* he thought, *"She's worked this entrance out a few times before, I bet!"*

"Gibson!" she gushed as she caught sight of him. She posed by the elevator to make her impression and also to make sure Gibson came to her. There was an air kiss and Gibson then guided her out the door, which had been opened by the liveried doorman as she carried on over how terrific Gibson looked while thinking, *"God he's aged! Has it been that long since I last saw him?"* In fact, Gibson was a handsome man who had aged a bit but was carrying it well. Think of Cary Grant in his later years. Strange how some men can age and, in the process, look more interesting, more attractive.

Gibson guided Dawna out the door and directed her toward the car as Gibson's chauffeur quickly rushed around to open the car door for her. As soon as Gibson was assured that his precious cargo was secured, he walked around to the other side of the car and got in next to Dawna. There was no need to direct the chauffeur where to go as Gibson had already briefed him. The chauffeur had already closed the window that separated the back seat from the driver's seat so Gibson and Dawna would have a sense of privacy as needed.

The drive to the restaurant took a bit more time than Gibson had expected, as traffic was even heavier than usual, but that was just fine, as he was setting a trap for Dawna and everything was at the ready. There was no rush. Gibson had laid out his attack to take place in Orso where Dawna used to hold court when she was in top form and commanding the attention and adoration of all of New York. True, she never quite got the attention that Richard Burton received when he did Hamlet on Broadway and Liz was in the audience.

Nor did she have the gimmick that Marlene Dietrich pulled when she appeared on Broadway. At that time, Alexander H. Cohen, Dietrich's producer, had arranged for Klieg lights to shine outside the theatre when she was doing her one-woman show so that huge crowds would gather after each of her evening performances. Surrounded by the Klieg lights, Cohen had a white Rolls-Royce waiting for her after the show just outside of the stage door and she would climb up using a special ladder and sit on the roof graciously taking programs from her adoring fans, signing them and then deliberately handing them away to someone else, causing the fans to fight over her signature. Gibson wondered, *"Cohen's gimmick with the Rolls-Royce was done in 1967 so maybe, just maybe, I could resurrect that trick and get away with it. An interesting thought."* Anything to promote his (hopefully) new star.

As the limo worked its way through the city traffic, Dawna took Gibson's hand and said, "So what have you been up to? I know you are a man who is always in constant motion, and I want to hear all. I'm all ears." That was just partially true. While Dawna wanted to know what was on Gibson's mind, she, as usual, couldn't help but eventually turn the subject toward her favorite subject: herself. Gibson was more than happy to play her adoring audience, even though his mind constantly wandered over to his planned attack.

And so, Dawna dove in. "I've been having the most wonderful time here in my favorite city. I've been seeing everyone and just catering to my every whim. I've been practically living at the Mandarin Oriental Spa, which is my special treat to myself after suffering all that time in the African jungle making my latest film. What a relief to be back in civilization! I'm wondering if maybe I ought to do more television work, as it is so less demanding and intrusive into my everyday life."

Gilson had heard via the grapevine how Dawna had managed to have in her contract that she was to be flown to her set in the jungle every day by helicopter because she insisted on staying at the elite and very expensive Ololo Safari Lodge located on the edge of Nairobi National Park in Kenya.

Gibson said, "I understand that you were housed at the Ololo Safari Lodge. It's lucky you have a discerning eye and to have made that arrangement," "*And a very smart agent to have made that deal for you*," Gibson thought to himself. "I fully understand your plight." "*Some plight*," he mused. "*That lady must be a handful. Change that to she'll certainly be a handful!*"

"But Gibson, the scenery, the animals! It was all so exotic, so… how would one put it into words? Well, you'll see. I'll bring you to a private screening when they get the movie all put together. Look at these wonderful bracelets," as she dangled a collection of exotic gold African trinkets in front of Gibson's eyes. "They were given to me at the end of the shoot. So beautiful and exotic. Perfect for me."

"*What an ego*," Gibson thought. "*But that's what I need. Someone who can take over a stage, conquer an adoring audience, and put an ass in every damned seat in the theatre.*"

"Now what have you been up to, Gibson? Tell me all."

"Ah, that's an interesting story, which I'll share with you over lunch."

Before they knew it, the limo pulled up in front of Orso and Gibson escorted Dawna up the stairs into the restaurant. She went down the three steps leading into the dining room, passed the reception area without stopping, and instead of going to her favorite table, which was just inside the reception area, she worked her way around the room, taking a circuitous route that led her past a number of other tables. As she passed by, she was greeted with "So nice to have you back, Dawna." "So good to see you!" "Dawna, you look marvelous!" "Is it true that you're doing a new television series?" and so forth.

Eventually, she and Gibson made their way to her favorite table and Gibson pulled out a chair for her, one where she could see the rest of the room and, more importantly, where everyone could see her. She rarely sat with her back to any audience. And so they settled into their table. Dawna had grandly made her entrance not realizing that she had walked right into a trap.

"Wonderful entrance," Gibson cooed, much to Dawna's delight. After casually draping her fur over one of the chairs, she eyed a pink package that had been set on it.

"Hmmm, I wonder what Gibson is up to and what's that package all about?" She thought.

They proceeded to order drinks: a lemon drop martini for Dawna and a scotch/rocks for Gibson, followed by some idle chitchat about a mutual friend who recently was making a big hit on a television mini-series.

"Did you see her latest facelift?" commented Dawna with a disapproving frown.

"When will some women learn to be happy with the face they've been given or at the very least to choose the right surgeon?" Gibson concurred and by a mutual unspoken agreement, nothing was mentioned about the few nips and tucks that Dawna had obviously recently indulged in.

Gibson then slowly worked around to the subject that Broadway missed Dawna and that "We've got to get you back where you belong." Music to Dawna's ears… a whole symphony.

"Did you see Lauren Bacall in Noel Coward's *Waiting in the Wings*?" Gibson asked.

"No," replied Dawna. "I was doing that sitcom at the time and never got back here to see it. Was she any good?" She had wanted to add "that dreadful sitcom" but would never demean one of her projects, even if it had a huge number of difficulties and really wasn't very good. Nevertheless, she was considerably richer because of it, and "*Oh, I love those residuals!*" she thought.

"Oh, it was kind of a disappointment in that Betty… that is, Lauren Bacall, was good in it," Gibson said. "How could she not be? But the show was never promoted properly. While I would have liked to have seen you in her role, I now have an even better idea. What I'd love to see is you wowing them in a musical, a variation of that show using a potpourri of Noel Coward songs." Gibson paused, letting his words sink in, and then added, "Just think, you, Dawna Drake, in a musical custom made for you with you charming the audience with your singing and dancing! We'll surround you with the best talent Broadway has to offer. That show will be made for you and only you!"

"One thing I should caution you about, when you read the script, don't get thrown by the fact that it sounds like it's a retirement home. While its location and purpose are similar to that of the Actors' Home in Englewood, New Jersey, we intend to downplay that aspect. Actually, I shouldn't tell you this, but Nicole Kidman was very interested in our musical and she's 56 years old, but she's like you, ageless. In any case, we will play down that retirement home aspect."

Gibson paused, watched Dawna's face like a hawk, and prepared to pounce on his prey as a smile swept over Dawna's famous and still amazingly beautiful face despite the fact that Dawna was about to turn 61. Gibson then proceeded to nail her with the comment, "I wonder if Marshall Ward would be right for the romantic male lead?" Of course, Gibson knew that Dawna and Marshall were secretly romantically involved. Secretly, except the whole world seemed to know about it; that is, all except Ward's wife, Carol.

"Enough said," commented Gibson. He reached down and picked up the pink package and presented it to her.

"Take this home and read it," he said. "It's a wonderful, really extraordinary vehicle called *Mad About the Gal!* that I feel is custom-tailored to your many talents. However, I warn you, don't dwell on the part of Valerie Lucile, your adversary in the show. While I plan to cast Clarrisa Roman in the part, the fact is with the music added, we don't need that role to be quite so extensive, so it will be cut quite a bit.

In a way, this was just perfect news for Dawna, as she had a long adversarial relationship with Clarissa and thought, *"Good, I can't stand that cunt and it will be great to get the better of her in public."* Dawna went on to fantasize about cowering Clarrisa into taking a "supporting" role credit or, better yet, having equal billing and then beating her out when the Tony Awards were handed out.

One of the things Gibson was counting on was the free publicity that Dawna and Clarrisa's long-standing feud would generate.

Putting those thoughts aside, regardless of how delicious they were, Dawna went to on to ask, "But won't this production cost a great deal of money?"

"Of course. Nothing but the best for my star, but leave that to me. Naturally, if you have any suggestions about potential backers, sing out," Gibson said with a charming smile, thinking *"And sing you will if I have my way!"*

And so, they chatted about the theatre, their mutual friends, and Dawna's favorite subject, Dawna. Lunch was minimal, partially because Dawna was always on a diet and, like Nancy Reagan, made it a practice of chewing a bite of food 20 times before swallowing it, thereby limiting her intake of anything that might incur damage to her still-famous figure. Also, she could not wait to tear into that script. Gibson too was anxious to leave, as he had a bigger need than food at the moment; he needed to raise the capital to finance this show now that Dawna appeared to be hooked.

While the original concept had been for *Mad About the Gal!* to be just a one-set show, kind of like Waiting in the Wings, this new production screamed to be "opened up" with some additional scenes that would require more sets and lots of costumes. Luckily there would be no chorus, as Gibson envisioned the actors depicting the residents of the home providing the singing and dancing. The challenge would be the casting of the show.

Act 1, Scene 2
Finding the Money

The next day, Gibson got a call at 10:00 AM from Dawna, which for her was "damned early."

"Good morning, Gibson" cooed Dawna.

"Well, good morning to you, Dawna. How's my star this morning? Did you get a chance to read that script?"

"Oh, Gibson, how could I not? It's full of humor and pathos, and while I have a few suggestions plus a few reservations about some of the songs, overall, I love it!"

Gibson grinned and fed the lines Dawna needed to hear. "Of course, you'll need a fabulous wardrobe." And before he could say anything more, Dawna butted in with, "I was thinking. Because my character would have wonderful taste and a great sense of style, maybe we could get Bob Mackie to do my costumes. I don't know which designer you have in mind, but

I simply must look spectacular."

Gibson thought better than mentioning that her character had seen better days and would not in reality look smashing as Dawna seemed to think she should. *Well, we'll deal with that later,*" he thought.

Dawna then said, "I know you producers always think of money and what things cost. I hope you have a good-size budget. Actually, I have a wonderful friend named Lilah Townsend who is simply swimming in money and is really quite interested in becoming a major backer of the show."

Clearly, Dawna had been a busy girl on her phone despite the hour. The one disturbing element came from Trish, Gibson's wife and co-producer. For some reason, she was adamantly opposed to taking on Dawna as the show's star, but Gibson had brushed aside his wife's concerns and forged ahead. This would eventually cause a great deal of trouble.

Act 1, Scene 3
A Second Trap is Set

Soon a meeting was set for Gibson to meet with Lilah in a few days, and another trap was devised. Gibson ascertained that Lilah had been a "great" friend of Betty Bacall, and it appeared that Dawna was taking over the role Betty had played in Lilah's life. Lilah even lived in the Dakota, the apartment building where Bacall had once lived. Gibson checked her out and learned that while Lilah had been socially dominant in past years, she had been ostracized when she was involved in a scandal involving a murder plot to kill her son-in-law and his son.

While Lilah had escaped prosecution owing to some high-end and clever lawyers, she nevertheless had been judged persona non grata by her socially prominent friends. Being a major player in a hit Broadway musical would do a great deal to restore her former status. Granted, her connections had been of a grander scale and had once included the Metropolitan Opera and the Metropolitan Museum of Art, but she was desperate to return to a position of power and influence among the rich. Being a producer of a hit show could be the perfect vehicle to make this happen.

Two days later, Gibson picked up Lilah with his limo at the Dakota. As with Dawna, he had the man behind the desk call up to her apartment, and in no time at all an elevator door opened and Lilah made an entrance of her own. She wore a fabulous array of diamonds: beautiful earrings, a large four-to-five-carat ring and a large brooch that Gibson was later to learn was a copy of one that Queen Elizabeth had worn. All this was set off by a simple black suit and a dazzling smile. Gibson stepped forward, took her hand, and said "I know you, I've seen your face in the society pages for a wonderfully long time."

Lilah shook his hand and said "And I know your face too. Everyone knows the famous producer Harold Gibson." In truth, Lilah had attacked her computer the previous day and had fully researched him.

"Then you know that everyone knows me as just Gibson."

As they chatted, Gibson ushered Lilah to his limo and, after he was seated next to her, his chauffeur drove them to Joe Allen's on West 46th Street, that well-known showbiz restaurant that catered to the famous and those who wanted to rub elbows with the famous. While it was a bit past its heyday, Joe Allen's still had a certain Broadway cachet about it. Upon their arrival, Gibson guided Lilah past the bar that lined the right side of the main dining room to their table in the back where they had a view of the entire restaurant with its walls covered with showbiz memorabilia.

They were seated immediately at the table with its immaculate white tablecloth and starched napkins as Arnold, one of the old-time waiters, appeared instantly. Legend had it that Arnold started work the day Joe Allen first opened his doors. Truth be known that was impossible, but legends were always rampant at Joe Allen's. Arnold asked if they would like to start with a drink. "I'll have my usual," Gibson replied. Gesturing to Lilah, he added, "I bet you're a Gibson girl. Ironic that my name is Gibson!"

To which Lilah said with a note of surprise and delight "You're right!" Gibson had done his homework too.

Gibson proceeded to explain to Lilah, "I know you've heard of this restaurant and have probably been here a number of times, but I wanted the chance to personally explain how it has a very special place in the Broadway theatre world. It was originally Joe Allen's town house, but he turned it into this famous restaurant. It also houses another restaurant called Orso, which I'll take you to. That's where you'll meet many famous Broadway celebrities. Joe Allen's has been here forever and is one of the favorite hangouts for many performers. You'd be surprised how many shows have germinated here… How many deals have been cut… How many stars have secured their spot in the Broadway world here and reaped their share of Tony Awards. Of course, this is not the hour when the place is really alive or full of the exciting Broadway scene. That typically is after eleven o'clock at night when the shows let out. I know you're fully aware of the Broadway scene but perhaps I can give you a bit of a different perspective about the business that you might never have come across. Through me, you'll begin to understand and appreciate this wonderful world as an insider. I'll take you here after we see a show one night and the place will be humming. You'll see and meet many of your favorite celebrities. By the way, are you free a week from Friday? I have opening night tickets to a new Broadway musical called *Better You Than Me*."

Lilah said, "Actually I have dinner plans, but let me see if I can move things around."

Gibson went on to say, "Excellent." Warming to his subject, he added, "Joe, while he was with us, was known for his wonderful sense of humor." Gesturing through to the next room, he said "Through that opening, there is a wall covered with show posters of notorious Broadway flops. Gesturing toward the wall Gibson said "There's *Kelly*, and also *Carrie*, *The Grass Harp*, Peter Allen's *Legs Diamond*, and *A Doll's Life*. Oh, and there's the sequel to *Bye Bye Bird-*

ie, a show called *Bring Back Birdie*, a real stinker. One of my favorite stories concerns the attempt to do a sequel to the huge success *Annie*. The show's creative team came up with *Annie 2, Miss Hannigan's Revenge*, starring Dorothy Loudon. The story goes that while out of town during the show's tryout, the producer came running down the aisle of the theatre during a rehearsal, screaming 'Everyone, get out of the theatre!' Miss Loudon, standing at the edge of the stage with her hands firmly on her hips, demanded: 'Why?' 'There's a bomb in the theater!' the producer replied. 'You mean there are two?' Loudon quipped." Chuckling, Gibson added: "Luckily, I'm not represented on that wall."

Gibson had tactfully called Joe Allen's the day before, spoke with Harry, who manages the restaurant, and asked if he would see that the three Gibson flops that graced that wall be removed "Just for today... I'll make it up to you."

Clearly, Lilah was impressed. "This is so exciting, so amazing," she gushed.

It didn't hurt that from time to time a few well-known stage celebrities came by for a brief "Hello." Lilah didn't realize at the time that networking was the life's blood of the Broadway theatre world and often the person coming over to say "Hello" was really just saying subtly, "Don't forget me when you cast your next show." It was even possible that Gibson had suggested to several actors that they might have lunch that afternoon, as his guest, and simply drop by his table to say "Hello." This scenario was working like a charm, as Lilah could barely contain her excitement. After the last actor left, she said, "Thank you for that introduction. I saw him last year in that wonderful Sondheim musical revival."

She thought, *I want to be part of this world. I wonder how I can join it?"* She was soon to find out as Gibson spun his web. He told her about this marvelous new musical based on Noel Coward's *Waiting in the Wings* to be called *Mad About the Gal!* "Your good friend Dawna is going to star in it and will no doubt take the town by storm." He elaborated on the creative team, saying, "To date, we have Allison Duprey, our show's director and the man who will guide our show, and, hopefully, Marshall Ward as Dawna's leading man. It's practically guaranteed to be a huge success. Our plan is to eventually bring it to London and then set up a national tour and maybe even take it to Japan. The show has no limits." Gibson had carefully used the word "we" so that Lilah would start thinking that she was part of the production team.

In fact, Lilah had had dinner the night before with Dawna and Marshall Ward and they had excitedly talked about the show. Lilah was getting more thrilled by the minute. By the end of lunch, Gibson had Lilah eating out of his hand. They left with Lilah having pledged to invest $3,000,000, "Or maybe a bit more," with the understanding that she would definitely get prominent billing as one of the top producers. Both she and Gibson left in an excellent mood as she had visions of winning a Tony Award to dress up her mantelpiece and having her reputation restored. Gibson, in turn, now had the seed money to launch his new show.

Later, after dropping Lilah off at the Dakota, Gibson went to work. First, he would need to have a meeting at his office to update the staff as to what was happening. Then, having secured the seed money, he would take out his trusty list of well-heeled friends and associates and start an endless series of phone calls, luncheons, and dinners to raise the rest of the money to mount the production. He thought $15,000,000 ought to do it and had already been working in his mind, assembling a team of writers and designers. It was always helpful to drop names of impressive players while making his pitch for financial backing. He knew every person he planned to call, and he would custom-fit his pitch to each recipient. He hoped to quickly raise the rest of the $15,000,000 to mount the show, as there would soon be many expenses such as endless casting auditions, as the show required a large cast.

It turned out that with rising costs due to the various unions, etc., the show's production costs would increase and Gibson would end up having to scramble to raise more money before he could hope to open the show on Broadway. In the meantime, he would also need to hire his production team, rent rehearsal space here in the City, secure a publicist to promote the show, hire the set, costume, and lighting designers, build the sets and costumes, rent the lighting equipment, promote the show, including the designing of lobby cards, and secure both a theatre out of town along with hotels and transportation, plus, of course, a good Broadway theatre.

The latter could be a problem, as his theatre needed to be larger than the Music Box but not so large as to make it seem less than a hit. One didn't want empty seats on any off days, yet it needed to be large enough to bring in enough money each week to not only pay the weekly expenses, but also to make money for the investors and, of course, himself. Gibson's plan was for the show to be a cash cow that would help defray the costs of running his very expensive offices and finance future shows. He wanted and needed a show similar to *Phantom of the Opera*, which had run for 35 years… a real challenge!

In the past, many shows had run for a nice period of time but ultimately lost every penny of the investors' money because their audiences were too small, or the theatre wasn't well located. One wanted to be west of Broadway. It was a complex and risky business with no guarantees. Having Dawna on board would help a great deal but would not ensure a hit. Few stars, if any these days, could provide such a guarantee and those who could fill a theatre night after night often demanded such large fees that the producer was hard-pressed to make his nut, that is, his expenses. Gibson was counting on Dawna's incredible reputation and popularity. But only time would tell if his gamble would pay off.

When Gibson got back to his office, the first thing he did was meet with his staff. He had called ahead and told his secretary what had to be done, and by the time Gibson had dropped off Lilah and got back to his office, everyone was gathered around the conference table ready to get to work. While Gibson had not told anyone what he was planning, everyone in Gibson's office was used to his fast, efficient way of operating, and they all knew he would expect long hours and complete dedication from his team. Gibson had a reputation for being a super-efficient and meticulous man. The story went that he once almost fired a new girl in the office for putting postage stamps on some outgoing envelopes crooked until he was talked into giving her a second chance. Everyone in the office was expected to be as exacting as Gibson. Appearances counted.

At the meeting, Gibson explained what this new production would be, and his team immediately caught his excitement. One of the secretaries commented to a colleague how lucky Gibson tended to be. Overhearing this, Gibson said, "Yeah, I've noticed that the harder I work, the luckier I get." To which his team nodded in agreement. Gibson was known to be extraordinarily focused, ambitious, and a hard worker. Heaven help anyone who got in his way.

And so there would be many more meetings, and numerous professionals would be added to "the Team," but this was a good start and with luck, it would represent the beginning of a significant theatrical production. As he had said to Lilah, "The show will hopefully sustain a number of touring companies as well as foreign productions. It will be a production we can be proud of." In reality, the show would keep Gibson's name in the game and his enterprise above water. Always a big concern. Not that anyone would realize it outside of Gibson's inner circle, but the reality was he desperately needed a hit!

Gibson started to finalize arrangements with various talented artists to create this new musical. In a less-than-inspired moment, the new production was titled, *It's Great, it's Grand!*, but later it was discovered that this proposed title had already been used for a cheap porno movie, so they eventually came up with a new title: *Mad about the Gal!*, nicknamed "Mad" for short in the office. The idea was to play down the old age home bit and instead make it a tribute to theatre history. "Mad" would introduce the younger crowd to a period of musical theatre before their time and simultaneously attract the older theatre-going crowd who tended to love the music from that era in theatre history.

Act 1, Scene 4
And the Production Took Shape

As the days got busier and busier, Gibson proceeded to secure the needed additional financial backing. He also secured a writing team since the original Coward production of *Waiting in the Wings* had been a flop in London and obviously needed a complete overhaul. Gibson settled on the writing team of Lefteris and Blom, two writers who, while talented and successful, had recently suffered a few failures and, like Gibson, needed a hit. So, Gibson was able to cut a sweet deal where the money they would make would come, mostly after the show was an established hit. Their job would be to take the old, tired Coward script, update it, and as Gibson said, "Give it a new, contemporary zip."

At his wife Trish's urging, Gibson cast Marshall Ward as the leading man after assuring Dawna that it had been her idea all along. This appeared at first to be a stroke of genius. Keeping the star happy was a big part of being successful as a producer. Keeping Trish happy was another job that Gibson took seriously. Theirs was a special partnership in which Trish knew Gibson so well that she could almost finish his sentences for him. However, the one flaw in their relationship was her inability to have children.

What he didn't know was that before they had met, Trish had become pregnant with an unwanted child and was forced to have an abortion that ended up being a butcher job and made her unable to ever again become pregnant. Her barrenness was the one sore spot in their relationship. He also didn't know that she and Marshall had once had a brief affair several years before he had met Trish.

A new concern soon developed. Despite the plethora of charming Noel Coward songs to draw on, many lyrics didn't mesh with the storyline. Songs like "If Love Were All" and "Someday I'll Find You" integrated moderately well, while others just didn't work at all. Faced with this dilemma and knowing that the clock was ticking, Gibson suggested that the production hire David Zippel, the gifted lyricist who often worked with Andrew Lloyd Webber and Disney. He seemed the ideal person to tweak and update the lyrics and possibly integrate songs not necessarily by Noel Coward. A meeting with Zippel was quickly arranged, but Gibson's timing was off. It turned out that

Zippel had recently agreed to start work on another project with Webber and would soon be working in London for several months. However, in an attempt to curry favor with Gibson and thereby keep the door open for future projects, Zippel recommended a new upcoming lyricist named Leonard (Lenny) Leith; a meeting was set for the next day, with Zippel graciously taking the time to attend and do the introductions.

Earlier, when Gibson had first conceived of the show, before he did anything, he got hold of Phil Waterson, who represented the Noel Coward estate, on the phone and said, "Hi, Phil. God, it's been forever since we've talked. Let's try to have lunch or a drink one of these days soon."

To which Phil replied, "Good to hear your voice. What's up?"

"This isn't for public knowledge and not for general publication, but I'm working on a terrific idea that everyone, including you and your organization, will benefit from. It's a new musical roughly based on Coward's *Waiting in the Wings*. But don't get too excited. The book is totally different. What I'm interested in is maybe, just maybe we might want to use a few of Coward's songs but with new lyrics. An exciting idea."

Phil said, "Oh, I don't know. Coward had a remarkable way with words. Let me think about that."

"Well, we don't have much time. We're on the fast track

here, and if we have to, we can easily go in a different direction. We don't have to use Coward's songs, It's just a charming idea."

There was a long pause, and Gibson thought maybe he had been disconnected. He was just about to redial when Phil said, "Oh, what the hell. Go ahead with this and we can work out the details later. I know you, you'll drive a hard but honest bargain."

And the two men, having basically agreed, hung up.

The meeting with Zippel, Lenny Leith, and Gibson and his team took place on the fourth floor of a rehearsal studio on 42nd Street. The room was plain, with a dull gray-green tiled floor, a nondescript table, ten or so gunmetal gray chairs, and a piano on wheels that had seen better days and had been rolled into a corner. Gibson took one look at the beat-up piano and thought, *"For what I'm paying for this rehearsal hall, the least they could do is have a decent piano."* But then, Gibson always wanted the best bang for the buck and appearances were very important to him.

Looking around the room he saw that the window on the opposite wall enabled one to look down on the 42nd Street traffic, and while it hadn't been cleaned for God knows how long, it was solid enough to keep the street traffic noise out. Leith showed up looking eager and a bit nervous. He was tall, well built, clearly familiar with a gym, maybe six feet one, and had dark wavy hair and intense eyes. He was very handsome. *"Hmmm,"* thought Gibson, *"I bet Dawna will want extra time with this guy. She'll eat him alive!"*

Zippel and Lenny had shown up just a bit before Gibson, and when Gibson arrived, along with the two book-writers whose job was to create a new storyline for the show, Zippel introduced the two in his usual charming way. Zippel had an attractive warmth about his persona that fit easily into most social and business situations. With a wide smile, he introduced Lenny to Gibson, saying, "Lenny, you're one lucky man. I would be astounded if you two don't get along like gangbusters." To Gibson he added, "You'll love this guy. He's very, very talented."

With that and almost on cue, the rest of the people who had been invited to the meeting started to show up. Gibson made the introductions. "Lenny, clearly you know David," gesturing towards Zippel, "But I want you to meet Allison Duprey, our show's director, and Lilah Townsend, one of our lead producers, and finally, here's Tad Morley, our musical director.

Everyone eagerly shook hands and smiled. That is, all except Allison, who shook hands but seemed a bit testy.

"What's that about?" thought Gibson. Gesturing toward Lenny, he said, "Now, let's see how everyone gets along, and

then hopefully we can sign you onto our team." At Zippel's suggestion, Lenny, to demonstrate his skills, sat down at the piano in the corner of the room while everyone gathered around and Lenny ran through three songs for which he had written the lyrics. They were, he explained, songs for a show that was currently an Off-Broadway musical called *She Should Have Said No*. There was no need to mention that the show was doing well. It was a colossal hit and everyone knew it.

Besides having a surprisingly charming voice, Lenny's smiles sold his words with amazing grace. *"If this is any sample of this guy's talent, he's going to save the day for all of us,"* thought Gibson hopefully. After hearing Lenny's three songs, Gibson said, "Clearly you have an ear for the type of material we're putting together." Then, getting Allison off to the side, Gibson said, "I like this guy. Are you ok with him?"

Allison paused, and then reluctantly nodded his head in agreement. Then Gibson turned to the rest and said," I think this guy is terrific and think he'll be a great addition to our team. Does anyone have any objection to adding Lenny to our team?" When no one objected, Gibson said to Lenny, "Let's you and I go to lunch and we'll work out the details of your contract and then you can call your agent. Welcome to the team!"

With that, Gibson took Lenny by the elbow and directed him out of the room. As they were leaving, Lenny looked back and saw a sea of stunned faces each harboring some very strong thoughts of his or her own.

And so, the obstacle of finding a lyricist appeared overcome, if not with some serious concerns and undertones of possible doubt. The next Tuesday a meeting was called in Gibson's offices to review the set and costume design needs. Gibson limited the meeting to Trish, who had a keen eye for spotting potential problems, Jens (whose real name was James Jenson but, as a theatrical set designer, he felt that Jens and just Jens sounded better), Elina Fay, who would create the costumes, and Fiona Williams, who would design the lighting for the show once the sets were OK'd, plus Allison, who had previously approved the design team. Gibson hoped that Allison wouldn't have a negative reaction to any of the designs once they were created.

Gibson had also invited Lilah Townsend, not because her presence was needed, but because Gibson still needed to raise more capital. Maybe, just maybe, he could involve Lilah to the point where he could hit her up for some additional funds. "You don't ask… you don't get," was his thinking. To date, Gibson had wasted no time and his lawyers had met with hers and she had already signed an agreement for her part in providing the promised $3,000,000. The money had been deposited into the show's account.

And so, they all met at Gibson's offices in the conference room with its severe décor in black and white including an over-scaled checkered floor pattern that always offended Jen's artistic taste. Gibson had once asked Jens what he thought of Trisha's decorating efforts, and Jens had been able to duck the question. Criticizing Trish was not a healthy thing to do. She was known to hold a grudge. The truth was, the office was a decorating disaster.

Long a fan of the now passé decorator Dorothy Draper, who had set the style for the Carlyle Hotel years before, Trish had decorated the numerous rooms in their office in white and black with out-of-date neo-baroque plaster decorations of busts and lots of heavy swirling headers over the doors and windows. Besides tiling the floor in that overscaled black and white checked pattern, she had used fabrics with huge floral roses that had been Draper's trademark. Eventually, Trish saw the folly of that and the fabric soon disappeared. Nevertheless, the overall effect was still bizarre and wildly dated.

Gibson said a few words about how well the production was "shaping up" and then asked Allison to talk about his thoughts on the production. Clearly having not given much thought about the production, Allison sidestepped the subject and dove into a discussion about Dawna's reputation for ignoring the creative talent on a production. "We'll have our work cut out for us, especially when it comes to the star's wardrobe," he said, and everyone nodded in agreement as they looked over at Elina with a touch of pity.

All in all, the meeting had gone very well. Gibson thought, *"This might be the last time everyone's in agreement, knowing how Allison works, which is often to pit one person against another. He's a pain in the ass but damn it, he's really talented and perfect for this production if our star doesn't kill him or if he doesn't kill her."*

Soon the meeting was over, leaving everyone with an odd mixture of optimism and pessimism. Optimism because to be in the business one needed to always have that dream of success, but pessimism because most shows never made their nut; that is, they made no profit at all. But it would work out one way or another. Only time would tell.

Next, Gibson got lucky. He was able to secure the Emerson Colonial Theater in Boston for an appropriate date to try out the show. It was a little sooner than he had hoped, but getting a booking into that place was a challenge at best. The idea was to rehearse the show in a studio in New York for six weeks and have several "invited run-throughs" at the end of the six weeks. The cast and production personnel would then move up to Boston, hold a tech rehearsal to set all the lighting cues, have a week of rehearsals on the set and finally run the show for two weeks with a paying audience in Boston before bringing it to a Broadway house.

Finally, with a sigh of relief, the Lunt-Fontanne Theater, a fine Broadway house on 46th Street, was confirmed. Once there, the production would hold a tech rehearsal, then previews with a paying audience for four weeks to test the show before officially opening in time to qualify for the Tony Awards. Finalizing the New York theater had remained a source of great concern for Gibson, but he finally nailed it when a show that had planned to move into the Lunt had folded out of town during its tryouts. Booking a Broadway theatre was a tricky and nerve-wracking business. In this case all positive; well, mostly positive.

On the negative side, there had been only time to fine-tune the script by staging just three readings of the show. Often, an incoming show would test the material by staging many more readings, which involved the actors usually first sitting in a partial circle and reading their lines from their scripts. Often this would be done with a small, invited audience without any physical action.

Later in a rehearsal hall, the director would "stage" the action indicating where he or she wanted the actors to move and when. This would be done in a rehearsal hall without any scenery, just props and the walls of the set marked out in tape on the floor. After a sufficient period of rehearsal time the production would be run with an invited audience. Ideally, this would happen several times to fine-tune the action of the show until the actors were ready to move to the tryout theatre. Overall, the schedule for this show was very tight and a considerable concern. If everything went smoothly, they would be fine. If not, who knew?

Meanwhile, endless auditions would hopefully locate the right actor for each role, plus understudies. Between Gibson and Allison, they blurred the age of the characters so they would be slightly younger; that way the actors could do the dance numbers eight times a week and survive and at the same time not cause Dawna to appear too old but, then again, not too young. The problem with Dawna was that she had an uncanny ability to project a younger persona than her actual age both on stage and off, and at 61, she was hell-bent to do just that on stage even if it went against what was called for in her character. Clearly, in Dawna's mind her appearance definitely came before any attention to her show's character.

While Allison and Gibson often did not agree on the casting of certain actors, they were savvy enough to each keep his opinion to himself when others were around. No one was aware that Allison in particular didn't approve of certain actors. But that was Allison… Never happy, never fully agreeable. And eventually, his displeasure would surface in an acidic manner.

The thing was, he had a talent for pulling such a large, complicated show together. He also, while often causing difficulties himself, had a nose for possible problems. As an example, from the beginning, he was opposed to the casting of Marshall Ward. Instinctively he sensed that Dawna would tire of him or resent his getting too much attention,

and "Once the ship had sailed we'll be in for a trainwreck…
Fuck the mixed metaphors." Trish meanwhile had cam-
paigned for Marshall, as she had plans of her own for him
to play in this production.

The day came when the show was fully cast with a total
of 18 actors, some of them doubling up and playing more
than one role. Thanks to some clever makeup, wigs, and
wardrobe, the audience would not be aware of this. And
so, the production was ready to move forward.

Act 1, Scene 5
And the Tension Grew...

In a matter of just three weeks, a designers' presentation had been scheduled, a very short and intense time as both Jens and Elina, while known to be not only brilliant designers, efficient and fast, had their work cut out for themselves. The tension was palpable. On the day of presenting their designs, all were gathered at Gibson's conference room. Jens had brought a model of the theatre in half-inch scale, and he was the first to present his work. It consisted of a handsome reproduction of the theatre's proscenium and backstage area including the set with all the magic tricks they would hopefully be able to afford so that the sets would not only be supportive to the show's storyline but be an added delight to the audience.

While Jens had won a Tony award a few years back for his outstanding sets for a production that took place in Renaissance times, he was realistic enough to know that no one would be leaving the theatre humming his sets this time around. He had come up with a basic set of the "home" where the characters lived.

To open up the set to move the action forward to portray the "show" set where the cast tries to raise money to save the home, Jens had the basic walls of the home set on two turntables that could revolve, one in a clockwise direction and the other in a counterclockwise direction, thereby magically turning the dowdy home into a glamorous ballroom. It was based roughly on Oliver Smith's original design for his *My Fair Lady* sets but, needless to say, Jens never mentioned this when demonstrating his design.

The presentation went fine until Jens activated the turntables. As the set changed, so did the audience at the meeting. While everyone had been nicely respectful of the "basic set," when it magically turned into the ballroom, Jens's design was met with great enthusiasm, even some light applause.

Fiona had a lighting question which was not so much directed towards a major issue but seemed to be more her way of making sure that she stayed very much a player in the production. Everyone seemed pleased with the way things were moving forward. Jens, of course, had discussed the colors he hoped to use for the set with Elina to make sure the sets and proposed costumes would work well together. As everyone knew, Allison could be a real bitch if he wasn't treated in just the right way at the right time. Jens had been around the block and knew the score, so he had secretly shown Allison his designs before the meeting this way, avoiding any public displeasure from Allison.

Just the week before, during a rehearsal, someone had muttered under his breath, "Allison as a child must have had his tongue caught in a pencil sharpener and it had stayed that way." Also, it soon became clear that the man had a drinking problem that sometimes led him to berate actors or other members of the show's team.

The day before, while rehearsing a scene, he had so verbally abused Sally White, one of the supporting players, that she ran out of the rehearsal hall in tears, and it took a considerable amount of cajoling to get her back in the room and functioning again. Allison thought nothing of calling her a "fat, ugly cow" in front of everyone. Needless to say, it was disturbing and offensive to most of the cast. But hey, Allison as the director was at this point in charge of the actors and had taken over much of the control of the production leaving Gibson to handle the financial end.

The actors, meanwhile, had to put up with Allison or do their best to avoid any confrontation with him.

He could be beyond charming when he wanted to be, but often he turned up drunk at evening rehearsals, as he was partial to evening rehearsals and the drinks he had during the dinner break. As a result, rehearsals could be hell. Strangely, he never verbally abused the stars of a show. He was nobody's fool, even when blind drunk. One night, however, he met his match. He had gone to dinner and had been drinking a great deal, more than his normal intake, which, needless to say, was considerable. He was getting into an elevator with two of the girls from the cast and when they realized he was so drunk that he didn't even recognize them, they nodded to each other and without saying a word, took off their high-heeled shoes and proceeded to beat him over the head with them. The next day, a very quiet Allison showed up at rehearsals with heel marks all over his head. He never was able to identify his attackers. *"There is justice in this world at times,"* thought a number of the cast.

Elina Fay's presentation of her costume designs was next and the several meetings with Jens had paid off. Both Jens and Elina had been trained at The Yale School of Drama and, as such, they stuck together. Some referred to this arrangement as "The Yale Mafia." In any case, the colors were right on and worked perfectly with Jens's color palette. Everyone seemed pleased, but all were aware that Dawna would have the final word on her costumes and, in reality, maybe about some of the other actors' costumes as well. Everyone was braced for possible changes to "suit our star."

During Dawna's last Broadway show, she decided that she didn't like her costumes and started wearing a ward-robe of her own choosing, which she bought at Gucci, Louis Vuitton, and Bergdorf Goodman. Moreover, she had the audacity to send the bill for the various outfits to the producer, whose hands were tied, as Dawna could decide to leave the show if she didn't get her way. "What could I do?" the producer reportedly had sadly said.

Jens quietly thought to himself *"Good luck, Elina, with Dawna. Hope she doesn't screw you…or all of us for that matter."* The meeting was finally adjourned. Later, when the costume sketches were shown to Dawna, she made "Just a few minor adjustments to better capture my character." Interesting how the word "few" can sometimes have different meanings to different people. Elina, having never worked with Dawna but well aware of Dawna's reputation, was VERY upset with her.

Once the sets were approved by Allison and Gibson, Jens's assistants quickly drafted up the set construction drawings and they were presented at a bidding session with three top theatrical shops: Hudson Scenic Studios, Global Scenic Services, and Adirondack Scenic Shop in Gibson's conference room. Jens had his assistants print up the needed number of blueprints of the set construction drawings and they were distributed to the men representing the three shops. Jens's assistants also set up the model of the show with special small lights that made the model look dramatic. One of Gibson's assistants had set up the conference table with coffee and doughnuts and the various shop representatives looked over the model, doughnuts in hand, and after a while, Jens started reviewing the construction drawing of set designs.

There were numerous questions regarding the time frame, where the sets would be first be set up (the answer being the Colonial Theatre in Boston), the nature of the turntables, and so forth. One of the men from Hudson Scenic took out his phone and started taking photos of the model and was promptly followed by the men from the other two shops. At the end of the session, Jens shook hands with the representative of the three shops, thanked them, and escorted them out of the office.

Over the next few days, Jens quickly fielded a series of questions from the various shops and after four days, all the bids came in. After reviewing them with the show's production manager, the associate producer, and Gibson's production supervisor, they selected Hudson Scenic as the best shop to build the sets and the show started to become a reality. Hudson Scenic had won the bid partly because it had suggested that the two large turntables be rented from a company called Theatre Techniques which everyone was familiar with. The agreement was that if the show was a hit and passed a certain date, the rental fees would be applied to the purchase of the tables and the production would eventually own the tables, thereby avoiding having to build the expensive turntables and also not have to pay for renting them for years and years. Everyone was happy with this arrangement. Meanwhile, everyone worked frantically to get the set designs into construction and shipped to Boston in time for the first performance. The tension was at an all-time high.

At the same time, Elina Fay quickly made the rounds with the costume sketches, along with swatches of the fabrics she wanted to use and soon got bids for the show's costumes. The one problem logistically was Dawna's wardrobe, which Dawna insisted "Must be built by Elizabeth Courtney", one of the top costume shops in the country located in Los Angeles. And while Courtney's was top-notch, Elina was furious at Dawna for demanding Courtney's as it made her work doubly time-consuming as she had to take several red-eye trips to L.A. to deal with the building of Dawna's costumes. Ultimately someone from Courtney's flew to New York to do the final fittings on Dawna. A total waste of money and her time in Elina's eyes. At one point Dawna had talked about possibly having Bob Mackie fine-tune some of Elina's designs but, luckily, that thought didn't go any further. Elina meanwhile was heard to mutter "I'll get even with Dawna if it is the last thing I do!"

Meanwhile, Fiona Williams started developing her lighting designs in the form of a light plot that would work both at the Colonial Theatre and at the Lunt-Fontanne. She got bids from companies that specialized in renting theatrical lighting equipment. The major difference between the two theatres was that the decorative drop that the audience first sees when entering the theatre could not be used in Boston. No problem; the lights Fiona planned to use for lighting the Colonial house curtain would work just fine for the drop that Jens had designed when they eventually got to Broadway.

And so, the day arrived when everyone in the cast was assembled for the first reading. With scripts in hand, each actor gathered around a large table and read out loud his or her lines so that everyone could get a feeling for the show. Allison announced that the singing of the musical numbers would be done by Tad Morley, the musical director, who would play the songs on the rehearsal piano. Later the actors would rehearse their numbers with Morley, and their musical numbers would be integrated into the production during the rehearsal process.

Morley looked impossibly young for the job, but at certain points in the script where an actor would normally perform his or her song, Morley sang the songs with a flash and dash that captivated everyone. Well, almost everyone. Allison was his usual dour self. Certain songs had not been assigned to specific actors yet and the competition to get those few plum songs created an undercurrent of tension.

Allison took delight in the stress present in the room. Quickly, the cast realized two things about Allison: with his lean, somber face that seemed to have a permanent scowl attached, his drinking exacerbated his evil and hurtful nature and he controlled the future of almost everyone in the cast. A dangerous combination.

Allison wasn't the only person to cause ongoing problems. Earlier, before even the first rehearsal when Dawna heard that Gibson intended to use Peggy Rand as the production stage manager, she was adamant that Peggy not be part of the production team. Gibson's response was, "Is there a problem?"

"Peggy was on one of my earlier shows," Dawna replied. "Let's say she was less than cooperative. Need I say more?"

"Sorry. What was the problem?" Gibson persisted.

"I'd rather not say."

So, all Gibson could do was shrug and think to himself, "If there's no solution, there's no problem." He ended up saying, "Sorry, Dawna, Peggy's deal is set and there's nothing I can do about it." Peggy somehow got wind of this conversation and when she heard that Dawna wanted her off the show, she was beyond annoyed, and Peggy had a reputation for getting even with people who crossed her.

The next topic: Dawna's dressing room soon came up. Something about the color of the walls needing to be "a certain beige-y pink". There seemed to be no end to the difficulties with Dawna, and Gibson wondered if maybe he had made a mistake framing the show around Dawna Drake in the first place.

On Day Three, when the various songs were slowly

being integrated into the rehearsal, the cast found Dawna very edgy. Gibson finally got her off to the side to find out what was bothering her. When asked, she shoved a note into Gibson's hands and said "Read that! How the hell did that get into my script?"

Gibson took the offered 4" by 4" white envelope made from a high-end stock with a card inside to match and pulled out a note with words printed in large green capital letters that said:

DAWNA
YOU MAY THINK THIS SHOW WILL
BE A TRIUMPH FOR YOU
BUT BEWARE, IT WILL BE YOUR DOWNFALL!
YOUR DAYS ARE NUMBERED!

Gibson read the note, then reread it and decided it was probably just a joke and nothing to worry about, but then thought: How did this get into Dawna's script and why is she taking it so seriously?

The next day, despite Gibson's reassurances, Dawna was still off. She had trouble focusing on the show. By the end of two weeks of rehearsal, her fellow actors were well on their way to knowing their lines, as the writing had a certain rhythm and was comparatively easy to learn. The same was true of the music. This was not the case for Dawna, who covered up her problem of learning the script and music by using a variety of excuses that fooled no one. She also had made a few enemies with certain cast members, as she insisted some of the less important actors and the crew address her as "Miss Drake." Only those in her "inner circle" were allowed to address her as Dawna.

As for Dawna not knowing her lines, Allison in particular was concerned and muttered something about "Some TV actors' performances are all smoke and mirrors and misplaced talent." Unfortunately, one of the minor actors overheard this and Allison's observation made the rounds in record time. The animosity toward the show's star was accelerated in ways that neither helped the show nor its star, and Gibson was concerned. Allison's comment about Dawna was of course nonsense, as Dawna was one of the rare ones who had won the big three: a Tony, an Emmy, and the Oscar and clearly was a gifted actress, but Allison loved to stir things up. He also loathed unprepared actors.

The next day, the principal actors were called in to start work on a few key scenes. If these scenes didn't work, there would be hell to pay and one never knew on whom the blame would fall. Would the parts of Lotta Bainbridge and May Davenport, now greatly changed and renamed Lois Rae and Valerie Lepage, come alive with Dawna and Clarrisa playing them, respectively? The next few weeks would be crucial. Dawna's having beat out Clarrisa for a Tony

Award eight years earlier actually helped, since the tension between the two ladies mirrored the hostility between their assigned characters. They arrived with a built-in resentment that promised to help define their roles.

The rehearsal halls for the show were in "The New 42 Street Studios" which was on the north side of 42 Street west of Broadway. It was common to see actors coming and going with scripts in hand, many with water bottles and an assortment of large tote bags and egos to match. A company typically took over several large rehearsal rooms equal to the size of a large Broadway stage, plus a smaller room for meetings or one-on-one rehearsals. Each room had numerous metal chairs, black music stands, and a piano. The latter, while usually beaten up with chips, scratches, and coffee cup stains, was regularly tuned and provided an important service. Overall, the rooms had little or no character, but that was soon changed when the actors arrived with their typical "larger-than-life" personalities.

Allison had his assistants call in Dawna and Clarrisa to explore the scene at the end of the first act in which Dawna's character confronts Clarrisa's and perpetrates a fight. Allison felt it should first be vocally confrontational but end up being physical. He wanted to be a hundred percent sure it would work between the two ladies. Consequently, he had the production company hire a well-known fight director named Felix Ruddner so the fight would seem real and the actresses could use some props in fighting each other but not get hurt. He toyed with the idea of having Dawna's character rip off Clarrisa's wig, but discarded that when he recalled a similar scene years before in *Legends* with Carol Channing and Mary Martin. In any case, he had to find some gimmick that would leave the audience gasping and talking about it during the intermission and, hopefully, after they left the theatre. What could that be? Then the ladies supplied the answer.

At 11 AM when the rehearsal was called, Clarrisa arrived exactly on time and with her part memorized. She was wearing tan and green slacks and a vibrant sea green silk blouse which accentuated her green eyes. The look was stunning and chic. Dawna arrived 15 minutes later with the excuse that "The traffic was hideous." She wore a cream-colored blouse with cranberry-colored slacks and exotic jewelry to match. Both ladies had been forewarned that there would be a fight captain at the rehearsal and that things could get quite physical. Clarrisa could easily move around in her outfit but it was questionable how Dawna would be able to maneuver with all her excessive jewelry, not to mention the long scarf that was partially pinned to her shoulder.

Dawna for some crazy reason had arrived with her dog Charma and her "personal assistant" Nat. The dog was ill-behaved and proceeded to bark endlessly. It soon became obvious that Charma was as spoiled and as out of control as Dawna, and soon the yapping dog was taken out of the rehearsal hall by Nat.

Clarrisa was considerably annoyed that Dawna had not arrived on time, not to mention that other bitch, Dawna's dog, and from there the tension built. Felix, the fight captain, worked with the two ladies after suggesting that Dawna take off her scarf, bracelets, and dangling earrings. It was interesting to try to distinguish the genuine hostility from the artificial. Felix had the two women grapple with each other, and even tried having them roll around the floor, but somehow it just didn't seem real or effective. And so, they stumbled through the rehearsal. It didn't help that Dawna knew neither her lines nor her character, which was ironic as all she had to do was play herself: a narcissistic, spoiled woman. *"Hmmm, typecasting,"* had crossed more than one mind.

Finally, Clarrisa got so frustrated with Dawna that she almost threw a cup of coffee at her during a break. Allison said, "Ah ha! That's it! We'll have Clarrisa's character throw a cup of hot coffee at Dawna." It was decided that the dress Dawna was to wear would be her favorite costume from a play her character had been in and that Clarrisa's character would throw coffee on her, thereby totally ruining the one memento that Dawna's character valued more than anything. It was up to Tony, the propman, and Roz, the head of wardrobe, to come up with a liquid that would appear to be coffee and look like it destroyed the dress, but in reality could be easily cleaned out of the costume. The problem turned out to be the temptation on Clarrisa's part to aim at Dawna's face but, being the consummate performer she was, Clarrisa aimed for the front of Dawna's dress. Tony temporarily came up with a large sheet of clear plastic and draped it around Dawna, so she was completely covered except for her face. "Clarrisa later claimed that the best part of that day was repeatedly throwing coffee at Dawna and once hitting her square in the face. "Oops," she said sweetly, "I'm sooo sorry," her voice dripping with insincerity as Dawna screamed and fumed.

"A perfect reaction on your part, Dawna," Allison beamed. "But Clarrisa, next time aim a BIT lower. Try to get it over her heart, wherever that is." He muttered under his breath for all to hear, including Dawna. Eventually Tony came up with some fake prop coffee and Elina worked up three copies of the needed dress that could be cleaned after each soaking of the coffee. If the show were a hit, more back-up dresses would be made.

Not to be topped in the "Demanding Actress" category, a few days into rehearsal, Clarrisa was stipulating that Tony "Find a prop chair with a seat higher than normal. I want the seat higher," she demanded, and even when Tony raised the seat several times, Clarrisa insisted "It just won't do." Clarrisa wanted control. She wanted her character to be above everyone, to which Dawna was heard to mutter for all to hear "She's right, Clarrisa should be in a highchair!"

And so it went, with Allison doing everything he could to keep the tension up between the two stars. It was an easy thing to do. "A real pleasure," Allison was heard to say with an evil grin.

Dawna continued to flounder, script in hand, somehow not quite getting a handle on her part, much less finding the nuances that would help to connect her character to the rest of the actors' characters. A resentment quickly developed on the part of many of the cast, who felt that Dawna, supposedly the STAR of the show, in capital letters, wasn't on top of her game. "What we need is a younger Meryl Streep or an older Kelli O'Hara instead of that un-professional bitch," Clarrisa muttered in a very clear voice intended to be heard in every corner of the two rehears-al rooms. Dawna acted as if nothing was wrong; however, stupid she wasn't.

The truth was something was distracting Dawna and she simply couldn't focus. It didn't help that Dawna's lead-ing man Marshall was completely pissed off at Dawna, as she was deliberately upstaging him. Often he made ungen-tlemanly observations about his leading lady. Seeing this, as one of the leading producers, Trish took Marshall aside and suggested that they have a glass of wine in an adjoining room after rehearsals were over.

Trish duly produced a bottle of wine and two glasses, closed the door, and asked "Still drink Pinot?"

When Marshall nodded yes, she poured two hefty glasses and launched into, "So how is it going for you?" knowing full well what was happening but wanting to hear him say it in his own words.

"You won't believe what a cunt your star has become. Boy, was I wrong about her. I used to think she was wonderful, truly amazing, but she's a bitch with a capital B."

Trish gave him a knowing smile, patted him on the shoulder, and said, "Well, you know she's been under a lot of pressure. Maybe she'll calm down." She said this with a certain sarcasm, knowing that Dawna and women like her never calm down. They thrive on the dramatic, the theatrical. So, Trish raised her glass and said, "Here's to a successful show and a good run for all of us. Especially a good time for you." After a slight pause, she added, "For us. Maybe even a replay of the good old days." She said with a smile, then downed the rest of her wine and left, but not before giving him a peck on the cheek.

"Hmmm," Marshall thought. "I've been so screwed up thinking about Dawna and myself, I've totally ignored Trish. I wonder… Could Trish be thinking of rekindling what we had long ago?" But that didn't help the problem at hand.

Soon Dawna started to ask, then demand, that Marshall's part be cut down, with line after line being either made shorter or eliminated altogether. At times Dawna took matters into her own hands. Ignoring Allison's staging directions, she would walk upstage so that Marshall would have to deliver his lines to her with his back to the audience. This created a degree of tension within the show that even Allison didn't want, but what could he do? If Dawna walked...

Gibson also had his hands full as he had to deal with the publicity people and the show's budget, which wasn't easy as Allison had expensive tastes. Allison was hinting that he might need to add a few more actors to the cast. "Maybe some younger dancers."

The one bright spot was Jens's idea to create two separate, inexpensive greenrooms (small, enclosed areas on either side of the stage where actors could relax when off stage, have a cup of coffee or tea, read, or talk quietly with other actors). Many of the actors who had lesser roles were assigned to dressing rooms that were one floor and, in some cases, two floors above stage level. These greenrooms would provide a place where actors, especially the older ones, could rest between scenes rather than climb up and down the steep and difficult steps in the middle of the show. This would work great in Boston but eventually not when the production reached Broadway.

Gibson also was concerned about the 14 by 22-inch show cards that were to advertise *Mad About the Gal!* He had discussed the cards with the three top advertising companies Serino Coyne, SpotCo, and Eliran Murphy Group who had the market for promoting Broadway shows well cornered. He settled on SpotCo to do the major promoting, knowing that they might well subcontract some of the promotional work out to the other two companies. After Gibson met with the folks at SpotCo, it was agreed that they would use a series of photos that Gibson arranged to have taken of the two stars of the show. He shrewdly had Dawna OK three of her photos and selected one of Clarrisa that SpotCo wanted to use and then got Clarrisa's OK for it. The ad company came up with ten different versions with various layouts and lettering styles and then when they were ready, Gibson had them set up in his production office and had SpotCo and a few of Gibson's trusted colleagues look at the selection; they helped him pick out the best of the batch. The poster everyone gravitated to was one where the two ladies were halfway facing each other and it looked like the poster was torn down the middle between the two stars. Effective, and it told the story. Gibson thought, *"Fingers crossed that this poster never ends up on that wall in Joe Allen's."*

Act 1, Scene 6
The Final Run-Through

And so, Allison worked on the show piece by piece, fine-tuning each performance and polishing the dialogue so the show would make sense and build. He continued to worry about the second act, which still was not as interesting as the first. Twice they had run the show in front of an invited audience and explored its strong and weak points. Before they knew it, they were into performing a final run-through of the show in the rehearsal hall with a small audience of maybe 125 friends, associates, and would-be investors.

Gibson had Jens bring in the model of the sets and place it on a tall table that Tony the propman had provided. Tony also arranged for 10 easels so that Elina could display some of her many costume sketches. It was fascinating how she captured the characters' essences in her drawings.

The purpose of the run-through was to see how the show played and, of course, there were some possible investors who, it was hoped, would help fill the coffers. What no one knew except Gibson and Trish was that they were still shy of the money needed to pull off the show. Years earlier, when David Merrick and Alexander H. Cohen were the major producers of their time, budgets for shows were reasonable. Producers didn't have to rely on lots of small investors and, consequently, could stand alone to accept a Tony for a show. Those days were long gone.

Now, thanks to the Unions and inflation, a musical could cost easily $10,000,000 to $15,000,000; one new musical in the works was rumored to be budgeted at well over $25,000,000! Securing the money for a Broadway musical posed a considerable challenge. Productions such as Gibson's were costly operations, and Gibson would have to share the glory with numerous secondary "producers," even if their contribution was as little as a quarter of a million dollars. That is, if he was lucky enough to win a Tony. Producing a musical on Broadway was a huge gamble with no guarantees.

After the audience took their seats, Gibson walked to the front to the sound of light applause. He held his hands up to stop it and then said, "Welcome to our wonderful musical. It's been an interesting journey so far and we have a ways to go. What you'll see today is special. It's our last performance before we head out of town to Boston, so you may see some rough edges here and there but by and large, I think we have a remarkable show and an amazing cast." Gesturing towards Peggy, he said, "Peggy here is our stage manager, and she'll describe the settings as we go along. There will be two acts with a 10 to 15-minute intermission."

Pointing towards the side of the room where the set model and costume sketches were displayed, he then said: "During that intermission, take a look at the model of the set and the wonderful work Jens, our set designer has done, and the imaginative and creative costume designs Elina has come up with. There'll also be some refreshments after the show for you to enjoy." Motioning towards Peggy, Gibson said, "If you please."

Peggy walked to the center of the staging area and said, "Our show takes place in two locales. The first act takes place in a home for actors and is filled with an assortment of interesting characters. Act 2 is set in a fabulous rented ballroom where the actors from the home perform a series of numbers as a benefit to raise money to save the home from being closed. As you'll see today, we have only props. The walls of the set are indicated by blue tape for the first act and red for the second. Enough said. Enjoy the show!"

With that, Tad Morley started to play the overture on the piano and the actors took their places. As he played, one could see smiles appear on the face in the audience. These were old, familiar melodies, and they were charming.

The first act went swimmingly. The songs had been well placed in the show and the new lyrics by Lenny Leith went over especially well. They were clever and amusing. Lefteris and Blom's book also played well, mixing humor with pathos. In no time, the audience began caring about the show's characters. But it was the fight scene between Dawna and Clarrisa that was the big surprise. Elina had whipped up a plastic cover that Dawna was able to slip on over her dress for her fight with Clarrisa. Tony the propman had devised some fake coffee for Clarrisa's character to throw and, as a result, the scene played extremely well, to everyone's delight. It was fun to see Dawna's character get her comeuppance and the audience loved it!

Again, the second act sort of just sat there… no real excitement. And while the key people connected with the show knew it needed work, no one was quite sure what the solution should be. It didn't help that Dawna still didn't know all her lines and wasn't in top form. The rest of the cast, however, was getting better and better and were all showing signs of being terrific in their roles. Maybe with a paying audience, in a real theatre, Dawna might rise to the occasion. Maybe… One could only hope. That little run-through did, however, hook two more producers, and the coffers were soon half a million dollars fatter. So the day was helpful in that area.

And so, time was up. The costumes had been made and fit, and, in Dawna's case refit, as the star fussed over every detail and then some. The scenery was constructed and lighting equipment delivered. Everything had been shipped to Boston, where the sets were installed and lit. The show was fully rehearsed and mostly ready to be tested out in front of a paying audience. So, after a few days off, the cast moved to Boston.

At this point, Clarrisa was enjoying a feeling of security in her role, although she was not happy about a few cuts Allison had requested. "How come Dawna's lines are never cut?" Clarrisa was heard to mutter more than once. Marshall was fuming and bitching under his breath about Dawna ruining his performance by upstaging him every chance she had, with Trish trying to calm him down. Allison was getting more evil by the day and was seen to hit the bottle at an accelerating rate, while Dawna, to put it mildly... SHE was not focused, was not happy, and was losing the respect of the cast at an alarming speed.

Lilah was into the production for a cool $3,000,000 but was thinking about investing more, as she was oblivious to the drama behind the scenes, as Gibson was making sure she was delighted with her new role as an "important producer." He shrewdly kept her busy planning where to hold the opening night-party. She, of course first focused on "getting a smashing outfit for the occasion." And then ended up booking Sardi's on West 44th Street, both the downstairs and the upstairs for the event, and could barely contain her excitement. She couldn't wait to invite those friends who had been less than warm to her after "that little incident with the burning boat" when she had been involved in the attempted murder of her son-in-law and his son.

While Gibson was more than pleased with being able to tap Lilah for some additional money, something bothered him about her, and after researching the scandal that had enveloped her, he made a mental note to keep an eye on her. After all, even though she had not been prosecuted, it was clear that she had tried to kill her son-in-law and grandson. In short, she could be dangerous and was certainly not to be trusted.

Little did anyone realize the dangers that awaited them in Boston.

Act 2, Scene 1
The Boston Tryout

Sunday, the cast and support team left for Boston and settled into their respective hotel rooms. The set, costumes, and crew had arrived ten days earlier at the Colonial Theatre, a grand old theatre in the best of traditions. It was overly large, maybe too large for the intimate moments in the show, but beautiful in an old-world manner and visually perfect for the tenor of the story. The cast, as instructed, reported to the theatre at 10:00 AM Monday and sat in the first three rows of seats looking at what was to be their new home for this new production. The cast had seen Jens's model of the set and thought it very nice, but this was different! There were so many little touches that said, "People really live here!" Fiona had arranged the lighting for the opening set of "The Home" to be warm and cozy. As a result, everyone was enthusiastic.

After Dawna arrived ten minutes late, Gibson stood at the lip of the stage and said, "Welcome to your new home, everyone. I have a feeling that you'll be happy here, as I suspect this set will be your home for a good many years." To which most everyone laughed and chuckled as a few just quietly smiled. "And now I'd like to turn the stage over to Allison." Allison moved to the front of the gathering and smiled. "Well," he said, "Here we go. As Gibson indicated here's your home away from home. It's up to all of you to make it special and to breathe life into it. In a few moments, you'll get to come up and explore the sets but before that, I'd like Peggy Rand, our head stage manager to introduce some of the team you haven't met."

Peggy quickly moved to the center of the stage and said, "Thanks, Allison. Doing the introductions will be my pleasure, as we have quite the stage crew. When I mention your name, please stand up so everyone can get to know you. First, there's Herb Adams, head carpenter." Polite applause. "Then there's Phil Dwyer, head electrician." More applause. "Roz Hanson, head of wardrobe, and finally Truett Connor, our key audio man. You already know Tony, our propman, from our New York rehearsals." Tony simply waved his hand, as the cast already knew him and were very fond of him.

"Now for the fun part. If you'll take those temporary steps over there to the left, please carefully come up onto the stage and check out the set… start to feel at home."

With that, the actors walked over to the steps, climbed up to the stage level, and wandered all over the set. There were polite murmurs as various actors walked through their entrances and tried out the prop furniture they had used in the New York rehearsals but now existed in the Real Home. Before the move to Boston, all the actors had to work with were walls indicated by taped lines on the floor.

The home had been named Rosedale, but in rehearsals, it was just a name. Now they had the actual thing. In many ways it made the play seem more real, more focused. But potential problems arose, such as how certain actors would exit from one area of the stage when they needed to make a quick costume change and then re-enter the stage from a different side. All this had to be worked out in the "tech," in which the actors went through the production one scene at a time as the lighting, sound, and props were checked out, and other technical concerns addressed. It was a tedious and lengthy process that could take many hours.

Dawna was having no part of it, except when it came to crucial moments when her exits meant getting into a different wardrobe. She demanded a stand-in "Like we do in television," and garnered yet more enemies, including Peggy, who was of the old school and believed everyone—including the stars—needed to be part of the tech rehearsal so everyone would be properly lit. "Fuck her," Peggy muttered under her breath. "What a stupid bitch. Without proper lighting, she'll look really old and it will serve her right!" Clarrisa, being a pro, stuck with the tech rehearsal all the way and made major points with the cast and crew. Overall, everyone was keyed up. Finally, things had become more real, and many of the cast and crew started to see that the show just might be the success everyone had hoped for.

As the stagehands changed the set from the home to the ballroom, one of those rare and truly creative moments happened. When Gibson and Allison saw how the set changed, they had the same thought. "This is too fantastic to happen behind the curtain during intermission. The audience must see this magic." What everyone saw was the ceiling fly out as the two turntables revolved, one clockwise and the other counterclockwise, and voila! There was the ballroom set. Pure theatrical magic.

After conferring with each other and being so pleased that they both came up with the same idea, they worked with Herb Adams, the head carpenter, and the crew, as well as with Fiona and her lighting cues, and with a few minor adjustments the transition from the home to the ballroom became a visual change for the whole audience to delight in. Best of all, it didn't cost Gibson a dime!

All that was needed was some transition music, which Tad Morley quickly came up with. It would take a day or two to score the needed music, but that was just part of the job and incurred no extra expense. The only additional cost would be a short rehearsal time with the orchestra that would be added to the schedule. Everything seemed possible at this point and very exhilarating.

The excitement spread throughout the company affecting everyone… everyone but Dawna. She seemed less than enthusiastic over the scenic effect and thought, *"No way am I going to be upstaged by some dumb scenery."*

So, Dawna fumed and marched off to her dressing room. She smiled as she looked at the color of the walls. She had requested that her dressing room be painted her favorite shade of "kind of a beige-y pink," which she felt went well with her skin tones. *"After all,"* she thought, *"If Yul Brynner had been able to have his dressing room painted chocolate brown, his favorite color, why shouldn't I demand to have mine painted the way I want it?"* And there it was, painted just like she had insisted it be. *"It's great to be a star and I have every intent to act the part,"* she thought.

Except for the proposed scenic move, she was generally pleased with the theatre and the show but was anxious about the upcoming dress rehearsal and the first preview performance, which was scheduled after the crew was finished teching the show. If only she could remember those fucking lines!

It was then that she had received those damned purple and green fake flowers and that infuriating note.

The next day, still upset, she reviewed her dressing

room and saw that Nat had set out a number of handsome live flower arrangements with accompanying cards declaring that the show would be a success and that she'd be a triumph, and so forth. Natalie Reynolds, or Nat as she was known, had been Dawna's maid and dresser-cum-confidante for about seven years and was well-adjusted to Dawna's demands and eccentric behavior. Later, Nat picked up the crumpled card from the floor and read it. *"Interesting,"* thought Nat. *"Whoever wrote that sure knows Dawna."* She then passed the note on to Gibson and Trish.

That day in her dressing room, Dawna discovered a gift that had suddenly shown up. It was a huge box of candy that came from a well-known chocolatier that Dawna particularly favored. *"Well, someone did his homework. I wonder who sent it?"* she thought as she opened the attached card. Again, the note was printed in green ink.

I TOLD YOU YOUR DAYS ARE NUMBERED
ARE YOU DYING TO BE IN THIS SHOW?

In a fit of pique, Dawna screamed at no one in particular, "What the hell is going on here?" She proceeded to hurl the box across the room, and the bulk of the contents spilled out over the floor. She then stormed out of the dressing room, slamming the door so hard that one of the framed photos of her popped off the wall and crashed to the floor.

Nat rushed to clean up the mess as Dawna went in search of her driver so she could let off some steam at her hotel. In her rush to escape, Dawna left her dog Charma behind, and Charma made a beeline for the spilled candy and ate as many pieces as possible before Nat shooed him away, knowing that chocolate is really bad for dogs. As Nat picked up the partially spilled box, she absentmindedly popped one of the candies into her mouth.

Dawna got into her limo that was parked in the back alley and demanded that the driver take her back to The Ritz Carlton. When she arrived, she passed through the lobby, ignoring the greeting from the hotel staff, and hurriedly got to her suite.

Three-quarters of an hour later, Dawna arrived back at the theatre considerably calmer only to find Nat being carried out of the theatre on a stretcher, groaning loudly, the sound of which was quickly drowned out by the wail of the ambulance siren as she was rushed off to the hospital.

Dawna needed two of those little white pills called Xanax to calm down. As she shook out the bottle, she discovered that she was down to just three pills. *"Damn,"* she thought. *"Just what I need, and with Nat in the hospital, she won't be able to order up a refill. Merde!"*

When Dawna reached her dressing room, she found a very dead Charma. Dawna's first thought for once wasn't about herself. It was about her dear dog, who usually went everywhere with her. "Oh, baby, what happened to you?" She cradled Charma in her arms and cried. It was only after some time that she started to worry about Nat. "What the hell is going on here? Maybe Peggy will know," she thought. Dawna gently put Charma down on the couch, put a towel over her body with her little head sticking out as though Dawna was putting her to bed, and then went in search of Peggy.

The sad thing was Dawna had lots of people whom she dealt with all the time… mostly to yell at, curry admiration from, or demand things of, but she had absolutely no one to confide in or anyone to comfort her except Nat. And she obviously was not available.

Meanwhile, Peggy had sent her assistant to the hospital to check on Nat, and it soon became apparent that Nat had food poisoning of some sort and was in intensive care. Dawna was terribly disturbed about the sudden death of Charma, but on the news of Nat's condition started to worry about how she would cope without her to keep everything running smoothly. Peggy was astounded that Dawna's primary concern was how she was going to cope without Nat and that she had not expressed any concerns for her. Seven years of loyalty to Dawna, or maybe that should be termed "putting up with Dawna's demands," apparently made little impact on Dawna's state of mind. She wanted her usual support, and she wanted it now!

Gibson was immediately drawn into the situation and assured Dawna that a replacement for Nat would be found "as soon as possible." Meanwhile, Peggy asked Roz, the head of wardrobe, to have one of her assistants take over handling Dawna's costumes. Dawna will just have to take care of her personal needs herself until a replacement for Nat can be found, Peggy thought coldly.

The doctors at the hospital quickly suspected that poison might be involved and alerted the police. Shortly, several policemen were sent to the theatre to investigate, but they seemed more interested in meeting Dawna and getting her autograph than investigating what had transpired. Eventually, the remainder of the candy was collected and sent to a lab, where it was determined that the candy had been laced with arsenic, a poison that would make a person very sick but was not usually lethal.

Dawna was shaken, but couldn't comprehend that anyone would want to kill her. And so, she quickly turned her attention to repeating her demands that a temporary replacement for Nat be found "As soon as possible—that is, until Nat gets better." Nat herself was released two days later and was undecided if she was literally dying to work for Dawna. Gibson offered to handsomely increase her salary, and she reluctantly returned to work a week later, making a point of eating out from then on, away from the theatre.

Act 2, Scene 2
Enter Inspector Willis

While Dawna fussed about being without a maid for a while, it slowly dawned on her that the note with the green printing might be serious and that maybe, just maybe, there was someone out there who for some unknown reason wanted her dead. *"Bizarre as that idea is,"* she thought. And so, she dramatically demanded that she have a private detective hired to "Get down to what the hell is going on here." Gibson's reply to Dawna was "Okay, Dawna, who do YOU suggest?" Dawna, remembering Lilah's connection with an Inspector Willis and his "3 In 1 Investigation Agency," suggested the firm be hired "At once!" Dawna had forgotten that Lilah was not on the best of terms with the Inspector.

That day an envelope arrived at Carol and Marshall Ward's

hotel suite addressed to Carol. Upon opening it she read in green letters:

**ARE YOU AWARE THAT YOUR
HUSBAND IS PLAYING DAWNA'S LOVER
BOTH ON AND OFF STAGE?**

Carol confronted Marshall with the note and said, "So those rumors are true!"

Marshall grabbed it, read it, said "You have to be kidding!" and stormed out of the suite. Soon he reached one of the Colonial Theatre's rehearsal halls, got Dawna off to the side, shoved the note under Dawna's nose, and said through clenched teeth, "Did you send this to Carol?"

Dawna read the note and got extremely upset. As she paced back and forth, she tore the note into as many small pieces as she could. In the process, she broke a nail and started screaming "Fuck, Fuck, FUCK!" Marshall thought that Dawna had freaked out over his wife learning about their affair. He had no idea that she was even more upset over the fact that the person sending the green messages was now hitting her where it could cause some real damage.

She might be cooling about her feelings towards Marshall, but she had no intention of having him quit the show and then having to adjust to a new leading man. Flexible she wasn't. Also, she wasn't a lady who had stayed on top of her game for a very long time without having well-honed survival instincts. She now had a feeling that the green messages might be more than she could handle.

The next day, Inspector Willis arrived along with his partner Ross at Gibson's New York offices. They were shown into the conference room with its antiquated décor. Gibson was finishing up a call with Dawna's agent. "I know Dawna's a needy star, but we're doing our best to promote both her and the show and it looks like we'll get a spread in "People" magazine coming up in a few weeks. Gotta go as I'm just going into a meeting. Bye," and he abruptly hung up.

Looking up at Willis, he said, "God, she's going to drive me insane! Why can't these stars be like Angela Lansbury and Bea Arthur were? Talented, sane, and fun?"

Willis smiled, extended his hand, and said "Hi, I'm Willis and this is Ross Langley, one of my partners."

They shook hands and each settled into one of the chairs around the conference room table. Willis looked around the room and noted the many framed posters from the numerous well-known shows Gibson had produced. *"Hmmm,"* thought Willis. *"I've heard of this man for a number of years. He's the modern-day version of the great Broadway producers David Merrick and Alexander Cohen. We'll see if this man lives up to his reputation."*

At this point, an attractive young lady entered with a tray containing two carafes of coffee (one regular and one with an orange lid that was decaf), cream and sugar, plus three white mugs that sported the name of one of Gibson's big hits on their sides, plus some small paper napkins. She smiled, set down the items, and asked "Will that be all?"

Gibson thanked her, and she left the room. He gestured towards the coffee and said, "Help yourselves." As the men each poured coffee, Gibson wasted no time and launched into the problem at hand. "We have a concern which, on the surface, could look like just a nuisance situation: a crazed fan who is trying to get some attention. In the summary I had my secretary send over to you I mentioned how that demented fan sent our star Dawna Drake some poisoned candy along with a threatening note in green ink. Fortunately, she didn't eat any of it but her assistant did and ended up very sick in the hospital. Dawna's dog also managed to eat quite a bit of the candy and died."

"Needless to say, our star is crazed with worry. This is a very serious situation as not only do we need to protect her, but we also need to find out who is possibly trying to kill her and why, so she can feel safe and can concentrate on her performance. We're into previews at the Colonial Theatre in Boston and I regret to say Dawna's performances to date have been less than stellar. Here's a copy for you of a list of the cast and crew. I've circled the ones in red who might for one reason or another hold a grudge against our star."

Willis and Ross looked at the list Gibson had given

them. Willis let out a low whistle. The list was awash with red circles. Gibson then went down his copy of the list:

"Marshall Ward—Dawna's leading man with whom she was having an affair. The relationship has gone south and he's very upset with her. She's not helping matters as she's doing her damnedest to upstage and minimize his performance."

"Carol Ward—Marshall's wife—could have gotten wind of Marshall's affair with Dawna and might be thinking of going to the press with her story. Of course, up to now few of the cast have seen her around the theatre, but she knows the doorman Harry, and apparently, she has dropped by to say 'Hi' to him. Overall, it appears that she has not been around the theatre much except for a visit or two, so it would be difficult for her to harm Dawna except through bad publicity, but she's a shrewd woman who has been known to be devious and vindictive. The last time she and Marshall broke up, she took him to court and was in the process of cleaning him out when they reconciled."

"Clarrisa Roman—the show's other star but not quite her co-star (in Dawna's mind.) We cast her because she's not only extremely talented, she's less than friendly with Dawna, having lost a Tony Award to her a number of years ago. We thought the animosity that Clarrisa feels towards Dawna would play well with the attitude of our characters in the play itself, However, we may have underestimated the degree of hostility that Clarrisa feels towards Dawna."

"Then there's Allison Duprey, our director, who's wonderfully talented as a director but someone who can be really evil in his treatment of actors. Most actors end up being terrified of him or just plain hate him. For what it's worth, he's been known to hit the bottle and to turn extremely nasty. I'm personally surprised that it isn't Allison himself whose life is being threatened. As for his attitude toward Dawna, he just barely tolerates her. No, the fact is he detests her."

"Interestingly enough, Nat, Dawna's dresser, maid, and assistant, has her difficulties with Dawna as well. Just before we moved to Boston to try out our show, I had quite the time convincing her to do the show. They've worked together for years, but apparently, their relationship has been getting more and more contentious. But of course, Nat was the one who got poisoned, so I guess that eliminates her as a suspect. Don't you think?"

"Of the creative team, there is Jens the set designer. His real name is James Jensen but he goes by just the name of Jens. He's done wonderful sets for the show and has a scenic change that the audience sees that's really terrific. He might just nail a Tony for it. Dawna has been campaigning to drop the scene change in front of the audience and have it happen with the curtain down during the intermission as it tends to upstage her. Jens is less than happy with her and this idea of hers. We tried to do a run-through without showing the scene change and the show suffered for not having that visual punch, so it's back in the show."

"We have a wonderful lighting designer named Fiona Nicholson. She's a detail lady and is doing a remarkable job but in truth, she despises Dawna for being unprofessional in that Dawna refused to participate when we teched the show, that's when Fiona lit the actors as they worked their way through the show. Dawna stayed in her dressing room and didn't do her job like everyone else. This might not seem like much to you, but the people on our creative staff are highly professional folks who eat, live, and breathe their work and anyone who interferes with their doing his or her job to the best of their ability is the enemy and is strongly disliked."

"Now Elina Fay, our costume designer, has had a particularly difficult time with Dawna in that Dawna thinks she knows everything about costuming and what's best for her. Dawna's not above critiquing Elina's designs for her wardrobe as well as the clothes for the other actors in the show. We're just into our out-of-town tryout and Dawna has already shown up on stage in an outfit she bought at Bergdorf Goodman's for her character's second-act entrance. I know this because she presented me with the bill for $5,300, saying that the costume that Elina had designed for her 'Just wouldn't do.' She said the original costume made her look fat! Needless to say, Elina is up in arms and just this morning bent my ear for half an hour ranting about Dawna and what a bitch she is and how she could kill her for what she's doing."

"I might add that Elina's feelings towards Dawna are not unique. Overall, everyone in the cast either really hates Dawna, dislikes her, or at the very least tolerates her. The reality is she arrived in Boston unprepared. She simply does not know her lines and has had to be prompted from the wings. Very unprofessional. Needless to say, that makes interacting with her character on stage very difficult for everyone. It throws everyone's timing off. But the bottom line is she sells tickets and is crucial to the show's success. We must find out who's threatening her… Who's trying to harm her. The fact is this list could and should include almost everyone connected with the show. I could go on and on. Never in my 32 years as a producer have I ever had such a challenging star. We're into previews now in preparation for getting the show ready for our opening on Broadway but thanks to our star, we're less than fully prepared. You two should come to Boston, see the show, and get to meet the cast. My wife Trish and I will be interested in hearing how you like our show and more importantly, having you two find out who is sending those damned green notes."

And so, Wallis and Ross left with their list of potential suspects, found a Starbucks, each secured a coffee and a salad, and sat down to discuss the case. As Willis pulled up a chair, he said "You know Ross, the fact is, we don't know if the perpetrator is thinking of killing Miss Drake or just trying to disrupt the production. As for Gibson and maybe his wife, what's her name?" he asked, snapping his fingers, "Trish… it's not beyond the possibility that they could be the would-be attackers. I bet that he has a large insurance policy on Dawna and that she could have an 'accident' that would pay handsomely and give the show some added publicity, too. I don't know enough about Gibson and his wife's business, but I'd put money on the fact that they could easily be the ones who might benefit from her death the most and might want to get her out of the way." Looking at Ross, he added, "How about snooping around when we get to Boston and find out what you can."

Ross nodded his agreement and said, "That director Allison sounds like a real piece of work. I wouldn't trust him. I've encountered people like him before and they can be dangerous. Let's keep an eye on him."

Willis then added, "And I don't trust our star. From what little we know, I bet Dawna could be behind this whole mess for God knows what reason. I wonder if all the bravado that we hear about her is just a shield so no one can see and know the real Dawna. Could be that all this is a play on her part for sympathy or publicity. Crazy, huh? Let's also keep an eye on the creative team. Sounds like there might be some big egos involved there as well."

"Oh, I just had a thought: do you think Marshall's wife

Carol could have sent the fake flowers and the poisoned chocolates?" suggested Ross.

"Interesting and quite possible," said Willis.

The more they discussed the situation, the more complex it got and the more fascinating.

Later that day, Wallis and Ross drove up to Boston to get a feel for the production and start interviewing the various suspects. Gibson's office called ahead and, using the show's rehearsal schedule, it was easy to get the times worked out for everyone to be interviewed. Peggy Rand was particularly helpful, as the schedule had changed two times already with the actors rehearsing during the day and performing the show at night. She was clearly a lady who was always on top of things. When they met backstage, she handed them the updated schedule along with two tickets to the show for that night. Willis and Ross were then directed to the DoubleTree hotel, which was conveniently near the theatre. Around 5:00 they grabbed an early dinner in the hotel lobby and, while eating, talked about the new job.

Ross started off the discussion with, "So, any ideas on how to go about this?"

Willis thought a moment and said, "There are so many folks who appear to have good cause to dislike Dawna, but trying to kill her seems a bit extreme. But then they might be overly theatrical and react to situations differently than you and I. This certainly will be an interesting case. I know that your brother Monty is currently tied up with his studies at Yale but would you keep him abreast of things as they develop? Maybe he'll come up with some thoughts." As Both men mulled over the situation, they finished up dinner and went over to the theatre to meet briefly with Peggy before seeing the show.

The Colonial Theatre was one of those fabulous old theatres that seated 1,700, had a large proscenium that appeared to be as tall as it was wide, and housed a grand drape that had been lit in a warm, welcoming red. Peggy met the men an hour and a half before the curtain was to go up and gave them a quick tour of the theatre and backstage area, plus filled them in as best she could during her limited time as it was a very busy period for her. She explained that the sets they would see that evening would be the same as those that would be used when they got to Broadway.

"The only exception was there would be no show curtain here at the Colonial as the theatre's proscenium or stage opening is far too large for the production's show curtain. In New York, the show will have a handsome drop to welcome the audience when they enter the theatre. The rest of the sets have worked out fine here but run a risk of getting a bit overpowered by the large scale of the theatre itself."

It was explained to the men, that Fiona, the lighting designer, had worked hard to focus the show so that it looked comfortable and inviting to the audience, a concept that was somewhat lost on Willis and Ross. Both men, however, noted that whenever Peggy mentioned Dawna, there was an ever-so-slight edge to her voice. Later, one of the actors would confide to Willis that Peggy had "…a bit of an ax to grind when it came to dealing with Dawna." Apparently, in an earlier show that they both had worked on, Dawna did something that highly offended Peggy. Why Peggy would take on a show with Dawna as its star under those conditions concerned Willis. Did she have any plans to "get even" with Dawna? crossed their minds.

For the moment, Willis decided that they would watch the show from out front in the audience but then see it from backstage tomorrow. As the auditorium filled up, Wallis and Ross took their seats and settled in to—hopefully—enjoy the show and learn more about the production. As the overture started up, they were surprised and pleased to find that they knew many of the songs, as the musical score turned out to be a collection of many classic, well-known pieces of music that had been adapted to the show.

It had turned out that the Noel Coward songs didn't work well in the production and the only song to make it into the show was "Someday I'll Find You". Luckily Gibson had negotiated with the Coward estate that their compensation would be adjusted according to the number of Noel Coward songs that ended up in the show.

The overture covered songs like:

"Getting to Know You"
by Richard Rodgers and Oscar Hammerstein II

"Where or When"
By Richard Rodgers and Lorenz Hart

"La Vie en Rose"
By Edith Piaf and Louiguy

"What'll I Do?"
By Irving Berlin

And numerous other similar songs.

The premise for the show was simple enough. The story revolved around a group of performers in a home for actors. In reality, it was a home for retired actors, but the production seemed to skirt around that issue so as not to make Dawna appear too old, and a good thing, too, because when she made her appearance, she was dazzling and looked very youthful. One initially wondered why she would be in what seemed like a retirement home at all, but soon she began to charm the audience and win them over to the point where no one cared. After all, beautiful actresses never seemed to look their true age.

The show came across as a vehicle custom-tailored for its star Dawna Drake. However, she seemed to have problems with some of her lines and was prompted from the wings in a way that most of the audience could hear her prompts and realize what was going on. Clearly, this was throwing the timing off for many of the other actors. It was not smooth sailing for anyone when their star was on stage with them but hey, it was in the early stages of the production's run. The formal opening wasn't scheduled for another two weeks.

Willis and Ross were enjoying the first act and then the big scene came up: Clarrisa's character has a big blowup with Dawna's and a fight ensues. It seemed VERY real and then, to the audience's surprise, Clarrisa took a cup of hot coffee and threw it at Dawna. The liquid went all over what the audience had been told was Dawna's favorite dress, one, she had used in her biggest triumph as an actress. And the dress looked like it had been totally ruined. As Dawna stood there shocked and obviously very upset, a single tear rolled down her cheek.

With that, the actors froze in position and the set magically started to move. The huge ceiling started to fly out of view as two turntables rotated and the retirement home magically turned into the grand ballroom that all the characters had been talking about. This would be the ballroom where they would put on their show to hopefully raise the money needed to save their home. It wowed the audience and there was a considerable amount of applause as the house curtain came down. The first act appeared to be terrific, and the show had the feeling of being a hit.

During the intermission, Willis and Ross milled around

the audience listening to the audience's comments. Mostly they heard people say how great it was to see Dawna in the flesh and wasn't she terrific although one lady said, "I wish I had been the one to throw that coffee. I just hate her character!" Another said, "I wonder how many dresses will be ruined doing this show?" "My guess is eight a week. Wow!" And then a man said "Isn't Clarrisa Roman fabulous? I'd hate to cross her character! I sure hope the second act is as good as the first." And so on. When the intermission was over, Willis and Ross returned to their seats interested to see how the show would play out.

The second act was okay, but just okay. The audience seemed to expect more, something that would top seeing the two ladies fighting, the dress getting ruined, and the magic of the home turning into a grand ballroom. But nothing exciting really happened. Sure, there were some fun performance pieces like Cora Williams as Francelle at the piano singing "La Vie En Rose" at a handsome white piano that Fiona lit in pink and surrounded it with projections of pink and red roses…. a charming moment. Then there was Clarrisa, who sang a beautiful ballad titled "What'll I Do" by Irving Berlin. Elina had put her in a beautiful silver gown with what appeared to have hundreds of small rhinestones, and, with Fiona's lighting, she shimmered and gleamed in a magical way. The lyrics were haunting and the whole impression was extraordinarily beautiful. After that, nothing in the rest of the act seemed special.

"Hmmm", Thought Willis, "They better come up with something to top that or Clarrisa will end up stealing the show."

At the end of the show there was a great deal of applause for everyone, but when Dawna made her entrance, even though her performance had been less than perfect, the place exploded. Apparently, no one cared that she seemed unprepared. They had seen Dawna Drake, an absolute star, in the flesh and they were wildly enthusiastic.

After the show, Willis and Ross went backstage. The actors had settled back to their dressing rooms to remove their makeup and get out of their costumes, with some of the actors briefly receiving friends or fans.

Willis wasn't sure how to take this, as it was unfamiliar turf for him, but he sensed that there was an uneasiness among the actors and the stage crew. Later, Gibson explained that an out-of-town tryout is like a maiden voyage or shakedown cruise. A tryout is often filled with a certain amount of tension and worry on everyone's part, as often, in the process of trying to make the show a success, an actor's dialogue might be enhanced or made shorter or even thrown out, and every actor is usually leery of changes where that individual actor might no longer shine. In short, each day brought changes, some that were welcomed and some that were upsetting.

After the audience had left and the actors were back in

their street clothes, there was a meeting in the first few rows of the audience where the actors and staff got notes first from Peggy and then Allison. Peggy started off by introducing Willis and Ross, explained why they were there, and asked that everyone be as cooperative as possible in helping them investigate the threats to Dawna. She then went on to give her notes to the various actors and design crew. When it came time for Allison to address the group, he was less than tactful with his comments and critiques. He was particularly brutal to several of the supporting players and the only comment directed to the stars was aimed at Dawna when he said, "Do you think you might grace this production by learning your lines? God knows you've had enough time." This was greeted by dead silence from everyone. Dawna started to say something then thought better of it.

During this time, Lilah sat a few rows back from everyone. While she was a major investor in the show, she clearly was not directly involved in the performance aspect of the production and so she hovered around on the perimeter of the action, observing. Every once in a while she would be tempted to make a comment or suggestion, but then would think better of it. She nevertheless was more deeply involved in the show than most people suspected. This did not go unnoticed by Willis, and he made a point of keeping an eye on her as he was extremely cautious about her. A few years earlier she had come close to being convicted for the attempted murder of Ross's brother Monty and Monty's father. That put Lilah on Willis's suspect list forever.

Eventually, Allison dismissed everyone. Many of the actors began to leave and Willis and Ross hung around a bit to see what they could learn. Ross overheard one of the actors say that some of the cast were going to a local bar across the street and down the road to the left. He suggested that he and Willis go there as they might learn more about what was going on. They soon found the bar which was called "The Blue Moon Saloon," a real nothing establishment with a tired-looking bar and with two bartenders to match.

The neon sign outside had the "N" burnt out so the sign read "THE BLUE MOO SALOON", and even though it was illegal to smoke in the bar, there seemed to be a stale quality to the air, as if people smoked there when the bar was officially closed.

Looking around, Ross noted that there were pockets of actors clustered together here and there, rehashing the night's work. Lenny was overheard saying how very pleased he was that the audience appeared to enjoy his lyrics, especially the show title song "Mad about the Gal!". It was terrific that the audience seemed to get the double entendres when the song spoke of how the singer was mad about the gal in that he was both crazy about her and furious at her at the same time. The same could be said of the cast and audience when it came to how they felt about Dawna.

There were also concerns about the dressing room ac-commodations and so forth, with Sally White chiming in, "Thank God for the two greenrooms that Jens built for us. Do you know where I would have to go between scenes if I wanted to rest without those greenrooms?" She asked. "I'll tell you, I'd need to climb up three flights of stairs and then listen to the intercom for the dialogue leading up to my next entrance! That is one outta-the-way place to rest but thanks to Jens, I can just walk 20 feet off stage and be comfortable. What a doll that man is!" With that, everyone chimed in, saying that the concept of having the two green-rooms on stage was a terrific idea.

Then someone mentioned Dawna, and the amount of vitriol was astounding. Here was a group of people who were in a show where the show's success rested mostly on Dawna's shoulders, and yet no one seemed to come to her defense. The big problem, except for her self-centeredness and lack of consideration for others, was her not knowing her lines even after all the days of rehearsal. "How the hell are we to pace the show and the laughs when there are those damned pauses while she waits to be cued?" muttered one of the ladies. And yet the audience loved her, which really annoyed a lot of the cast.

No one mentioned the threats to her life, as that was a gray area where there was little or no information out there.

But of course, there was tons of gossip and rumors. Everyone seemed to love the moment when Clarrisa throws the coffee on Dawna, thereby ruining her prized dress. Willis took mental notes of all of this and tried to get a clear picture of what was really going on. This theatrical environment didn't seem realistic to Willis and therefore, it wasn't easy to get an accurate understanding of what was going on. Were the comments and complaints of the actors valid or just a bunch of people being overly theatrical, acting out their frustrations and insecurities?

Willis and Ross were also surprised that Allison had joined the cast at the bar. They had heard that he had a reputation for a being a bit of a loner and not one to socialize, but he liked to drink and liked it a lot and this bar was convenient! The more he drank, the looser he became… also, the meaner. He was in one corner of the bar ranting about the state of the theatre in general and the condition of *Mad about the Gal!* in particular.

It was not a pretty scene as it was clear that he was mad at one particular Gal, and that was Dawna. "How the hell am I to pace this fucking show when there are those impossible pauses when that cunt needs to be prompted?" he snarled. "Poor Truitt in audio is going ballistic trying to balance the audio sound so that the audience hears the actors but not when Dawna is being cued from the wings. The fact is, no one in the audience, even in the back row can miss hearing that. Shit! How she's ever been able to perform on stage is anybody's fucking guess. If I had only known…" and he left it at that.

Shifting his attention away from Allison, Willis thought, "It wasn't that bad. I only counted five or six times when she needed to be given her lines." He then reviewed in his mind his meeting with Dawna late that afternoon.

At first, he was dazzled by her beauty. Yes, she wasn't a young woman, but she had an allure that only a mature woman might have. Close up, she was simply amazing with her flawless skin, beautiful red hair with its blonde highlights, and astounding body. No wonder she was the spokesperson for a well-known beauty product line. Her beauty was based on her elegance, intelligence (when it came to acting), and, unfortunately yes, her arrogance. Willis was impressed. At one point, he even asked her "Who do you think might want to harm you?" He had deliberately avoided saying the words "to kill you" as he instinctively knew she might not fully comprehend that possibility. As it turned out, she simply could not accept the idea.

"How do we know that there was really poison in that candy?" she asked lamely. "Maybe it had just gone bad." It appeared that she lived in her own world that only included situations that fit terms she could deal with.

"*A fascinating woman, but certainly unrealistic and from what I've seen and heard. Not nice, not nice at all,*" he thought. Willis had finally asked Dawna directly, "Who do you think sent the poisoned candy?" Dawna floundered around for an answer that would satisfy Willis and fit a concept she could live with, but ended up not being able to answer his question.

Rubbing his chin, Willis thought to himself, *"If she doesn't or can't help us solve this situation soon, she might very well be a dead woman before long."* Willis was right about the seriousness of the threat to Dawna but at the moment devoid of any leads as to who the perpetrator might be.

Over the next few days, new material was added that was stunning and immediately successful. What happened was, as part of the story, there are two lawyers who arrive at the home towards the end of Act 1 and announce that the home will soon be closed due to lack of funds to support its upkeep. The occupants decide that they will put on a benefit show to raise the needed funds. They go into staging this show knowing that it will be next to impossible to raise all the needed money, but the actors bravely push forward. Just before the finale, they learn that someone has anonymously donated an enormous amount of money… The home is saved and they end up finishing up the show with a big finale number celebrating the new-found largesse!

For the new finale, Kevin worked up a wonderful dance number where the entire cast dances to a variation of Coward's "Mad About the Boy" but with new lyrics by Lenny which were fun and fit the show to a tee. The number now was "Mad About The Gal!"

The theatre, while a good size for a musical, had a limited orchestra pit that was all but eliminated by the set's stage platform that projected out over the orchestra pit. The musicians were therefore relegated to the theatre's basement, along with the prop, electric, and wardrobe departments. This enabled the production to have several trapdoors and elevators built into the stage floor so that at the end of the fund-raising scene and the end of the musical itself, Dawna could make her special finale entrance.

What happened was: a hole in the floor opened up and she was lifted out of the basement on an elevator that would continue rising through the opening in the stage floor and continue upwards so that Dawna would end up on a pedestal-like platform that would be a good eight feet above the stage floor. The cast would then dance around her as the show built to a huge finale. All very effective. Added to the number were four strong male dancers who appeared without shirts to show off their ripped muscles. Why musclemen would be connected with a fundraiser was questionable, but the home had its contacts and friends so the four men had "volunteered" to help out. Their job in reality had been to add youth to the production and boost up the ending of the big finale. They were to act as adoring fans of the star, Dawna. The addition of the four male dancers added greatly to the effectiveness of the show, but it put a big dent in the show's budget and caused Gibson some sleepless nights worrying about how to come up with the money to cover this new expense.

Two days later, during the Saturday evening performance and at the end of the first act when Clarrisa's character hurls the coffee at Dawna's character, the liquid turned out to be real coffee and very hot! Dawna's look of astonishment and anger surpassed any reactions to that bit of business in her past performances. She was livid and burnt. No single tear this time!

Act 2, Scene 3
What Next?

Gibson immediately canceled the usual after-performance note sessions and called an emergency meeting in the greenroom for a specific few. Peggy announced over the intercom that the room was to be off limits to everyone except those who were summoned to the meeting. Included was Dawna, not because she would be of any help but because it was essential that the star feel she was being heard from and cared about. Also included were Allison, Clarrisa, Trish, Tony, the head propman, and Roz the head of wardrobe, plus Willis and Ross. Lilah had wanted to attend but clearly had not been invited, much to her annoyance.

Right off the bat, before anyone could say anything, Roz launched into a tirade, screaming "What's going on here? That costume is meant to only have fake coffee on it so it can be successfully cleaned. How the hell did real coffee get thrown at Miss Drake? That costume is ruined, and we only have three copies of it." She said this while glaring at Tony the head propman. In fact, everyone stared at the poor man who was clearly upset.

When everyone quieted down, Tony said in a small voice. "Someone tampered with the prop coffee. Just as I was setting it out to be carried on to the set by Clarrisa, I noticed that it looked odd. It wasn't the fake coffee I had placed in the cup earlier. I took a sniff of it and it had a very strange chemical odor. Not wanting to take any chances, I grabbed a cup of coffee from one of the greenrooms and put it on the tray. Gesturing towards Dawna, "I'm sorry that the coffee was so hot, Miss Drake." Turning back to Willis, he said, "I've just come from the prop room and I don't understand. The prop coffee seems to be an acid of some sort. Some of it spilled onto the prop table in all the fuss of replacing it and the area where it spilled appears to be somewhat eaten away."

There was dead silence. Everyone began to comprehend the seriousness of what might have happened if Tony hadn't replaced the "coffee". All one could hear was Dawna quietly sobbing. Willis quickly said, "Whatever you do, don't touch that cup of acid. I'll need to have it dusted for fingerprints and have the contents analyzed." After a long pause, a very sober group of people slowly got up and left the greenroom.

Back in Dawna's dressing room, she found an envelope with her name on it and a note inside in green block letters that read:

ENJOY YOUR PERFORMANCE
WHILE YOU CAN…
AS AN ACTRESS, YOU'RE ABOUT
TO TAKE THE ACID TEST!

The next afternoon during rehearsals, while Allison fine-tuned various scenes and the performances, there was a strange sober atmosphere in the theatre. Gone were the usual exciting conversations, the buzz that normally would be there in anticipation of the opening night. Even Allison seemed to ease up on his demands of the actors. Everyone was processing what had happened or, should it be said, "What might have happened and yes, what next?" Dawna got very quiet. Although she finally was learning her lines, her performance was now strangely devoid of any star quality. There was no excitement, no electricity. In fact, there was no excitement backstage. It was as if everyone was holding his or her breath waiting to see what would happen next. Consequently, the audience was less connected too, which had Gibson and Allison very worried.

Later the next day, Dawna and the cast were reassured

when three uniformed policemen were stationed around the theatre. One on the stage level, one in the basement and one in the theatre audience. It was a very effective move which gave Dawna and the rest of the actors the much-needed feeling of safety they desperately craved. However, when Willis questioned Gibson about them, Gibson reluctantly confessed that when he went to the police and asked for protection, he was told, in no uncertain terms, that such police support was not possible. The attitude of the police was unnerving in that they gave Willis a choice: either he solve the problem himself or they would shut the show down, as they claimed that they didn't have the manpower to put on the case.

And so, to help control the situation, Gibson went out and hired three actors and sent them to a local costume house to get the uniforms. It wasn't a great solution, but he had to do something to calm the actors down. Trish thought the idea was brilliant. Willis less so, but he had to admire Gibson's chutzpah.

The following day was a matinee day, and that morning Willis was walking past Clarrisa's dressing room and noticed that her door was open. He peeked in and saw Clarrisa sitting, absent-mindedly thumbing through a magazine. Clearly, she was comfortable with knowing her lines and appeared to be quite relaxed. Willis knocked on the door and as she looked up, he asked, "Would you mind if I come in and chatted with you a bit?"

"Help yourself," Clarrisa said, gesturing for him to take a seat on the couch as she cleared it of some magazines she had obviously been reading. "How's it going?" she asked as Willis sat down.

"It's a little too soon to tell, but I must say this show has a collection of some very interesting people. How's it going for you?

"For me… fine." she replied. "I wouldn't mind a bigger part but what I have is fun to play and I'm already getting the responses I want."

"Have you been acting very long?" Willis asked rather innocently, having checked her bio on the internet.

To which Clarrisa replied, "All my life or so, it seems. If you have four or five hours, I can tell you about it." Seeing Willis's reaction, she replied, "Just kidding, but really it's kind of a long story."

Willis looked at her and was immediately interested as she looked like a fascinating woman.

"Tell me, Clarrisa, how did you get started in the business?"

She responded to his question by taking a long pause and then said, "Ever since I can remember, people fussed over me. Back in Toledo, people would say, 'How pretty you are. You should be an actress,' and so forth and so on. So, I was pushed into school plays and community productions. Really, it seems like it's been what I've done my whole life. It also turned out that's what I've always wanted to do. As a child, my mother was determined that I would be perfectly trained, perfectly prepared so that when I got what she called 'My big break,' I'd be ready. That meant I took lots of ballet and classical dance training along with tap and ballroom plus vocal lessons. I also started going to acting school, which was kind of a joke as the woman who ran the school was a total fraud. She really didn't know how to teach acting at all."

"Luckily, I seemed to have a natural talent for it and so when I was 14, Mom dumped Dad and she and I moved to Hollywood. My mother was very controlling, very ambitious. I wasn't allowed to date. Hell, she was a piece of work. She had given me the name Clarissa which was misspelled on my birth certificate as 'C-L-A-R-R-I-S-A.' She put in the double 'R's' when there should have had double 'S's' as in 'C-L-A-R-I-S-S-A.'"

"Anyway, I eventually liked using that unusual spelling of the word as it made me feel kind of unique. I soon landed a part on a soap and consequently an agent. I was kept very busy with that role plus numerous commercial jobs. Finally, I had enough! I quit the show and my mother. I refused to let her interfere with my life from then on. The big question was 'Where to go?' Ultimately, I went to Las Vegas and managed to land a job in the MGM show *Jubilee*.

I was only 17 and had to lie about my age as the legal age to perform was 18 but hey, a friend helped me get a false ID and they believed it. As for the job, 'Easy," I thought. I'd just parade around with my tits out. Ha! Was I wrong! For the job I took on, one had to be an athlete. Besides needing to be at least five feet eight inches tall, which I am, and being able to dance, you had to wear three-inch heels as well as some really heavy costumes. The weight of the costumes was mostly in the headdresses, which often weighed over 20 pounds. You also needed to know everyone's routines so that if someone was out sick, you could cover for that person. It was grueling, but hey, I was young, ambitious, and strong! And I loved my independence, I might add."

"At the end of my contract, I took a job on the road with a famous male singer—who will remain nameless—and his band. My job was to dance around him and dress up the production. All I'll say is he was similar to, say, Frank Sinatra and Julio Iglesias in that he was a real ladies' man. The tour took six months and, among other things, I learned was how to defend myself. He never got into my pants and I'm kinda proud of that. After the tour was over, I went to New York with a girlfriend who knew some people… agents and such. I was in many ways still a bit naïve, but strong and perhaps misguidedly convinced that I would be a star."

"Well, it didn't happen as fast as I thought it would and, to put it succinctly, after two marriages and several abortions and many years of hard work, I finally had learned my craft and got a really good part in a fine Broadway play for which I was nominated for a Tony. I didn't win, but the nomination brought me a lot of attention. The important thing is I still love the business and I now know that I'm really good at my craft. I deserve to be where I am today and hopefully, I'll get the type of recognition I firmly believe I'm entitled to. Do I like every aspect of the work? Hell, no. Do I like working with the likes of Dawna Drake? What do you think?"

Before Willis could answer, Clarrisa said, "You bet your ass, I don't. I detest the way she showed up here in Boston without knowing her lines. It makes playing comedy very difficult, as one's timing is thrown off by the damned pauses when that bitch needs to be prompted. The fun part is she's not very savvy when it comes to acting on stage. For example: when an actor sets up a line for another actor to deliver a joke, if the actor who is setting up the line for the other actor moves just a little after delivering his line, the audience's attention stays with the actor delivering the set-up line, thereby lessening the impact of the joke. It's an old British stage trick and Dawna hasn't a clue when I do it to her. The sad thing is, she's actually quite talented and certainly has star quality. It's just that besides not being very smart on stage, she's an unprofessional bitch and I don't have an ounce of sympathy or respect for her."

With that, Willis heard Peggy's voice come over the speaker in Clarrisa's dressing room announcing: "Half hour everyone, half hour!" and Willis thanked her for her time and wished her a good performance. The question was: had Clarrisa just given Willis one of her better performances?

After the matinee, Willis went to Marshall's dressing room and knocked on the door. When he opened it, Marshall appeared somewhat surprised and disappointed to see Willis.

"I wonder who he was expecting?" Willis thought. Willis noticed that Marshall, while still a handsome man, was showing signs of wear and tear. It was clear that he was in the process of pouring himself a vodka on the rocks and he asked Willis what he'd like to drink. Willis settled for a diet soda, which Marshall got out of the small refrigerator in the corner of the dressing room. Willis then asked if they could talk a bit and the two men settled in for a chat.

"First off," Willis asked, "How are you holding up?" Willis had learned over time to ask a question or two that expressed concern for the person being interrogated. This often helped open up the person and enabled Willis to ask more direct, personal questions as the conversation deepened.

"I'm hanging in there, but I can't say this is the best time in my life."

"What's been the best time in your life?" Willis asked.

"Oh, there have been lots, as I've had a wonderful career… at least up until this show. Strangely, one of the best times was when I landed this job. I was so excited to be performing with Dawna Drake. She has such a name you know. Now, I have all sorts of names for her. She's unprofessional, egomaniacal… She's a sexless cunt." The latter made no sense at all as the one thing that was consistent with Dawna was her sexiness.

"Why is that?" asked Willis, putting on the best innocent act he could.

"Either you're blind or maybe you haven't been here long enough. Dawna Drake is the most impossible, unprofessional bitch I've ever worked with."

"Putting that aside for the moment," Willis said, "From what I've heard and also from reading your bio in the show's program, you appear to have had a wonderful, exciting career to date. How did you get started?"

Marshall thought for a while and then said with a sly grin, "It was a fluke. I had never thought of acting. I was very into sports when I was growing up and was particularly good at football. While playing in college I was recruited in my sophomore year by a sports scout and began having quite a professional career. There was an article about me in Sports Illustrated magazine and a theatrical agent saw a photo of me and liked my looks. The next thing I knew I had an agent named Tritt, short for his last name Trittipo, who had a lot of clout. He was famous for his insight and instincts when it came to spotting potential talents. He signed me up, a guy with no acting experience at all, and it all somehow clicked. That's it in a nutshell. The weird thing is I had a talent that I had no idea existed within me. Tritt got me lots of small bits here and there and because the camera apparently loved me, I got away with some really mediocre acting, but over time I slowly learned this new craft and I sort of built a name for myself."

"I gained quite a following while working on a big soap opera. On a lark, Tritt had me try doing some summer stock during a break in my role on the soap and to everyone's surprise, including myself, I was good. Acting in front of an audience was for some reason an excellent fit for me. So, I left the soap when my contract was up and did more and more acting in plays and eventually musicals. Along the way, I had some fun times, made some excellent money, and married Carol, a very nice, understanding woman. Maybe that's an understatement because we've been separated twice, but somehow we've always gotten back together."

Returning to the meat of the interview, Willis asked, "So how's it going on this show?" knowing full well what Marshall's answer might be.

"If you're asking me how I'm enjoying working on this show, I'd have to say it in some ways it's the low point of my career. I'm stuck working with the worst bitch ever. I could kill her…" He laughed at that last comment of his and said, "It looks like I have company in that department. Sounds like there's someone out there who wants her dead more than I do."

Shaking his head from side to side, Marshall muttered, "I'm just plain miserable. At the moment, Carol is really not talking to me, and I have just a few friends here in the show. Not the glamorous life everyone thinks it is, and I'm at a loss as to how to fix it. I feel like I've been sentenced to two years of hell until my contract is up."

Willis didn't learn much more. Marshall appeared to be someone who felt trapped, who hated Dawna, and seemed to be at a loss as to how to fix his life. Willis thanked Marshall for his time and asked him to let him know if he saw anything suspicious. In the meantime, Ross had checked Carol out and no one seemed to have seen her backstage at the time when someone had replaced the prop coffee with acid to be thrown at Dawna.

Later that evening, after the matinee and before the evening performance, Trish knocked on Marshall's door and entered without waiting to be invited in. He was just stepping out of the shower and had wrapped a towel around his waist. Trish looked him up and down, sort of playfully shrugged, and said, "Lookin' as good as ever." She closed the door behind her and locked it. Trish always wore a handsome string of pearls and she often subconsciously fingered them when she was nervous and she obviously was now.

Marshall stared at her for a long time, then quietly but firmly said, "Come over here."

Trish smiled and said "I tell you what, how about meeting me halfway?"

They both smiled and met in the middle of the room and embraced. Neither said a word as their tongues explored the old familiar territory but with a newfound interest. Trish took hold of Marshal's towel and, taking both ends, pulled on them, forcing Marshal's body up against hers. Her clothes got wet from his body, but she couldn't have cared less.

After all the years, they were once again together and the released tension in both their bodies was replaced by an intense passion. As they kissed and embraced, Marshall suddenly swept her off her feet and carried her to the chaise next to his dressing table and proceeded to revisit that which he had been missing for so many years. Meanwhile, the company continued to fine tune the musical without noticing that there was a new duet added behind the scenes.

Act 2, Scene 4
And the Show Settled Down

Strangely, as time passed, there were no more mysterious green notes. Slowly things seemed to somewhat settle down in preparation for moving the show on to Broadway. There was a feeling that maybe this had all been a bad dream, as the feared attack from the would-be assailant never seemed to materialize. Nothing. Maybe the presence of Gibson's "police" had helped. There were no more notes, just an eerie silence that was, on the surface, calming but also strangely unnerving. Slowly, Dawna learned her lines and in doing so, started to build her character. She was disturbed, however, when several of her friends who came to see her show said that she looked "tired" on stage. Her friend Lilah also voiced that opinion. And so, Peggy had to have a special crew call to fix Dawna's lighting and this time Dawna was there so Fiona could properly light her. Meanwhile, the other actors worked hard at improving their performances as Allison shaped and formed the show. With each passing day, the show got stronger and the threat to Dawna seemed to fade into the background. One was tempted to think it was all just a bad dream… and then the review from the Boston Globe came out and it was insightful in that it said in part:

Harold Gibson, one of Broadway's top and long-lasting producers, has brought a new/old musical production built LOOSELY around an old Noel Coward play, *Waiting in the Wings*. Revamped with a new title *Mad About the Gal!*, the show has a cast of superb professionals who have given credence to a Coward play that originally was mediocre at best.

This show now has the story line enhanced with a potpourri of fond, older songs, some with new lyrics by wordsmith Lenny Leith, who has invigorated these all-time favorite songs with a new vitality that adds life and wit to a show that can use all the help that time and money can buy.

With a bit more work, Gibson may well have a considerable hit on his hands. Which brings us to the star of this show, Dawna Drake. Beloved star of film, television, and theatre, she is beyond good, she's wonderful, make that sensational! Besides bringing a wealth of talent and experience, she somehow has brought a unique quality, which despite her many abilities, has up to now eluded her. In her role of Lois Rae, an actress of many facets, she sings and yes, dances with skill and charm but more than that, she brings a mysterious vulnerability to her role as though her life is built on eggshells… A person who is delicate and imperiled, but determined to survive. She is amazing!

Countering her performance is her adversary, Clarrisa Roman, who plays Valerie Lepage, a force of nature of her own making. You will delight when you see her try to pull Dawna's character down a notch. No, you will do more than that, you will cheer her as she does to Dawna's character what we all would like to do to anyone we know who deserves a comeuppance. I won't spoil the surprise but what she does is DELICIOUS and that's just the first act! It gets better. Adding to this is set designer Jens's contribution, which does the impossible. He tops two extraordinary actresses at the top of their game with a scenic effect that has the audience leaving the theatre humming the sets. It will be interesting to see how this show, which is still trying out its wings, will evolve as it flies its way to Broadway. Will Dawna's character prevail? It's anyone's guess. Here's to a soaring and brilliant flight."

—Maurice Zuber
The Boston Globe

And so, everyone was up on the show and settled in to work hard to make it the best they could. Dawna started to fine-tune her character and grew into her performance. She was no slouch and given the correct script and opportunity she could turn in a masterful performance and that's what began to happen. The company would typically work each day dealing with changes to the script and the increasing demands of Allison who, regardless of how well the show was shaping up, started to increase his intake of alcohol and was getting more demanding and meaner by the day. Slowly, but surely, everyone had a feeling that they might have a show that was extra special and that a huge hit was within reach.

As the show shaped up, so did Willis's and Ross's understanding of the problem at hand. For a while, there were no further interruptions on the part of the would-be attacker. The first assault had been with a poison that could have seriously attacked Dawna's health but not kill her, and the second attack appeared to be an attempt to wreak havoc with the relationship between Dawna and Marshall by clueing Marshal's wife Carol as to what was going on between the two actors off stage but that almost seemed inconsequential, as the two had been clearly drifting apart as it was.

The third note involved the acid incident that would have seriously disfigured Dawna had Tony not been so alert. Would there be more attacks and if so, what form would they take? It was imperative that Willis find the perpetrator and find him fast before Dawna and the show got hurt.

Interestingly, the focus of the company turned more and more towards securing the status of the show being a hit and conveniently putting the assaults on Dawna out of mind. Even Dawna got so distracted working on her performance that the attempted assaults on her faded somewhat into the background. But not so for Willis. He sensed that the would-be assailant was just biding his time and that soon enough he would show his hand, and Willis intended to be ready for him.

As time went on, Willis and Ross worked their way down the list of suspects. The first person they had interviewed had been Clarrisa who, while cooperative, did nothing to hide her hostility towards Dawna. Clearly, they had a long-time feud going on, but it was also obvious that Clar-risa valued her responsibility to deliver a good performance regardless of her lack of respect for her co-star. She dug into her character and was heard to say, "I don't give a rat's ass if someone is out to get Dawna. There's a long line of folks who want to nail her but, truth be known, she may be a shit in life but she's finally doing her job and delivering a good performance." Willis in turn admired Clarrisa's honesty and felt that she probably wasn't a real danger to Dawna.

As for Gibson, he seemed to be riding high on the show as the box office and was doing excellent business, especially after the review in the *Boston Globe*. However, with a bit of snooping around, it became clear that he and Trish were heavily invested in their need for the show to be a hit. If he were to lose his star through some sort of accident, all might be lost, and that just didn't make sense.

As for the insurance policy: did it cover an injury or—worse yet—the death of the star if it was perpetrated and not an accident? An interesting question. It turned out that Gibson admitted that he was in negotiations with the agent of "an excellent standby star," but he would not reveal her name and she and her agent would not make a commitment until she saw the show and the opening night reviews came out.

After interviewing Marshall, Willis arranged to talk to Nat. After the brief stay at the hospital, she had taken a few days off and was now back dealing with Dawna and her ever-increasing needs. Nat readily agreed that Dawna was high maintenance, but then the two ladies had worked together for years and had a rhythm when it came to dealing with each other. Their interactions were at times challenging but ultimately manageable. Nevertheless, Willis kept thinking that there was the slim possibility that Nat might have taken a small dose of the poison herself to alarm Dawna and also divert any suspicion away from herself. Nat came across to Willis as a shrewd character who had a love-hate relationship with Dawna. *"Complicated,"* thought Willis.

As for Allison, while he drank to excess and was extremely nasty to others, harming Dawna would ultimately hurt him in the long run. As Gibson had pointed out: if Dawna was to leave the show, there was a serious question if a bankable replacement could be found in time. When Willis questioned Allison about this possibility, Allison said that he had heard that Gibson was already on top of this and was in the process of getting someone as a stand-by/understudy for Dawna, but that Gibson was very tight-lipped about who this might be.

"Maybe Gibson is bluffing about getting a standby to replace Dawna," Allison said with an evil grin. "The problem is without the show having opened on Broadway with credible raves, it'll be very hard to find someone who is bankable as Dawna's replacement. I would like Nicole Kidman, who at 56 years old is a bit too young but is capable of playing any age. "Unfortunately, there's no way Meryl Streep would consider replacing anyone. But there are others," he said with a shrug. Then as an aside he said, "Streep will probably nail the part when they eventually make a film of this show."

Later, at a quiet moment backstage, Ross cornered Peggy Rand, the head stage manager. "I've been meaning to ask you about your relationship with Dawna," he said bluntly.

Peggy, somewhat taken aback, thought for a moment and finally said, "Okay." She let out a long sigh. "There's no one in the greenroom now so let's go there and talk. What I have to say is between you and me and not to be discussed with the rest of the cast. Agreed?"

Ross said, "Agreed. What you tell me is just between the two of us and, of course, Willis."

They went into the greenroom and, as Peggy had indicated, it was empty. They settled into two comfortable chairs. Peggy took a deep breath and then said, "To say that Dawna is a complicated woman would be an understatement and possibly misleading. She really isn't complicated in the normal way, in that she is totally focused on just one thing and that's 'Dawna Drake.' In quotes." As Peggy said that, she made quotation marks with two fingers in each hand. "She's totally absorbed with herself and often can't comprehend that others don't share the same fascination. She fully believes that everyone should be entranced by her. A few years ago, she and I were working on the same show. Unfortunately, the audience and the critics were not entranced with her or her performance and she was, needless to say, very upset and needed as much support as possible. And that's part of my job. Things, however, got a bit complicated. It's not necessarily common knowledge but I'm gay. I have a great partner, but I keep my private life separate from my work."

"Well, as you probably had surmised, Dawna is nobody's fool and while she might be overly obsessed with herself, she also has an antenna when it comes to evaluating the people around her. So, there she was with a show that was not supporting of her ego, and she looked around and saw me and thought. 'How could I not fall for her charms?' Well, as I said, I have a great partner and I was not only shocked, I was also definitely not interested. I bet you can guess how that went over. She does not deal with rejection, not at all. I'm personally a bit surprised, no, make that totally amazed that she didn't put a stop to my being hired as the head stage manager on this show. Maybe Gibson was able to set my deal before she could object. Who knows? Anyway, she and I have been very careful around each other. I have no ax to grind when dealing with her but I'm not so sure about her. While you're at it, you also might take a good look at Trish. She has an interesting background and has more to do with this production than you probably realize."

Willis then asked, "Care to elaborate on that?"

To which Peggy raised her two hands, slapped them on her thighs, and said, "Nope." And that was the end of their conversation. With that, Peggy excused herself and went to check on "A problem with one of the wigs."

A few hours later, Willis and Ross decided to follow up on Peggy's suggestion and arranged to meet with Trish. She seemed oddly distracted and claimed the reason was the great stress everyone was under. "Normally putting a show through the creative process is difficult at best, but with all this business of Dawna being attacked by God knows who, it ramps up the stress level."

As she talked about the show and its star, Trish played with her pearl necklace and tended to look around nervously. She finally said, "You'll have to excuse me, but as Gibson's wife and fellow lead producer I have a great deal on my mind. This is a crazy time for all of us. I don't want to be rude, but I'm really very busy. Lilah has just asked to see me, god knows what she wants! I'm sorry, I probably won't be much help to you."

Ross, wanting to milk Trish for as much information as he could, quickly said, "This won't take but a few moments and it will help us a great deal. We're curious, how did you ever get into this business?"

Trish sighed and, realizing she needed to cooperate with Willis and Ross, settled into a chair and replied,

"Strange you should ask that, as few people do. Most assume that being Gibson's wife, I'm just kind of an attachment, a hanger-on, but I really have been connected to the theatre business all my adult life and even before that, and I know it inside and out. I started out as kind of a tech-type person, working in summer stock theatres doing rigging, lighting, painting sets, and so forth. Theatre has been in my blood from my teens on. I just loved it and I was amazingly good at it. I thought I might end up being a lighting designer, as that field has a lot of women in it. You know, the rigging, the focusing of lights, breathing beauty into an environment that would have no life without creative lighting. And then I met Gibson, and everything changed. He taught me to look at the entire picture, how to put a show together, how to, you know... well, maybe you don't. Producing shows is a difficult, incredibly demanding, and stressful job, but when one gets a hit, there's nothing like it."

"How do you feel about this production?" asked Willis.

"I'm tempted to say it's driving me crazy with the stress, the egos, and yeah, those darn green notes. I wish I fully understood the motivation behind the hatred Dawna is getting exposed to, but then I don't understand our star." As she said this, Trish nervously played with the pearl necklace that she always wore. One of the actors confided to Ross that Gibson had given it to Trish as an anniversary gift and they were natural pearls and believed to be worth between $40,000 and $50,000. Willis thought, *"Those pearls look real and very handsome. I wish I could say the same of her hair color."*

Trish went on to say "I sometimes think that Dawna is her own worst enemy and brings on all the negativity upon herself. It's hard for me to explain."

"What do you think will ultimately happen?" Ross asked.

Trish thought for a split second and said, "I think the bitch will die!"

Both Willis and Ross were shocked, and Trish seemed somewhat surprised by her response as well. She ended up saying, "Forget that I said that. I'm just so stressed out. As we all know, Dawna is not a very likable person. With that, she looked over her shoulder, and said, "You'll have to excuse me, Gibson wants me to make some calls and I've been putting them off, which is not a good thing to do. It's sometimes hard to stay focused these days."

Both men looked at each other and mulled over what they had just heard after Trish hurried away. Later that afternoon as rehearsals continued, Gibson cornered Willis in the balcony of the theatre.

"So, how's it going, Willis?" Gibson asked, gesturing down to the actors below on the stage.

Willis noted in his mind that they were almost like gods looking down on the action below as the actors were being put through their paces by Allison. Kind of a strange sensation. He then replied, "Slow going. This is one interesting collection of people you've gathered here, to say the least. Amazing that they can function and put forth a united front when clearly most of them have little or no respect for the star."

"I regret to admit that what you just said is the understatement of the year about the cast's feelings towards Dawna, and yet you have to admit she brings something special to the show. She's a unique conundrum and, quite truthfully, a mystery to me as are most great stars. What makes them so distinct… beats me. One can't ignore the fact that she's in a very special class of those who have earned the triple crown in showbiz: the Emmy, the Tony, and the Oscar. She's extraordinary."

Willis nodded his head in admiration.

After a pause, Gibson went on to note "Isn't it interesting that you and I both go by just our last names? Unusual…"

Willis had to agree, but wondered if Gibson's observation was an attempt to bond the two of them in a way that Willis would take Gibson off his suspect list.

"Tell me, Willis, how did your company form and how did it get its title? I'd really like to know."

"Well, that's a change of subject," thought Willis. "Do you want the long or the short version?" he asked.

"Up to you. Your choice" quipped Gibson.

"Three years ago, I was faced with a curious crime. Monty, one of my partners, the guy who's attending Yale, was in a boating accident along with his father Ben Anderson. The boat mysteriously caught fire and Ben was reported missing and presumedly drowned. His body hadn't been found. Monty was able to swim to shore and was understandably beside himself and I was the police inspector who was attached to the case, hence my handle Inspector Willis. A really fascinating story in itself, but maybe some other time. I'm not much for talking about myself. In any case, it was a clear case of arson and there were a number of potential perpetrators. Ironically, there was a surprise element that popped up. It turned out that Monty, unbeknownst to himself, had been adopted and also had a twin brother out there whose name is Ross, who is my other partner and whom you've met."

"Anyway, it was a complicated crime, but between Ross, Monty, and myself, we solved who the culprit was… who firebombed the boat. You might be interested in knowing, if you haven't already heard, that Lilah was initially accused of being involved with the attempted murder but got off the hook thanks to some very smart lawyers. If I were you, I'd be super cautious around that woman. She cannot be trusted. Amazingly enough, Ross, Monty and I really hit it off. I never had kids of my own, so I kind of adopted the two of them. Around that time, I had been thinking about retiring from the force, so we decided to form our own company, hence the name "The 3 in 1 Investigation Agency." I think you'll find that Ross and his brother Monty, who you'll eventually meet, are both extremely bright. Together, we've already solved a number of crimes. That said, we feel that we'll find the perpetrator of these attacks on Dawna. My only hope is we can solve the problem before she gets hurt."

"Interesting," said Gibson. "I hope you solve it sooner rather than later, or we won't have a show and I'll lose my shirt and possibly my marriage, as Trish is going wild with worry. She's at the point where she's at times just not making sense, she's so worried and concerned."

Willis wondered if Gibson added that comment about "losing his shirt" as a means of saying, it can't be me as I have nothing to gain by Dawna's death or, at the very least, her not being able to perform in the show. *I need to check out what sort of insurance Gibson has on Dawna regarding her life or her inability to perform in the show.* Willis paused for a moment and then thought, *"What the hell, I might as well just ask him."*

"Let me ask you a question," said Willis. "I assume you have an insurance policy on the show and especially on its star. Am I correct?"

Gibson paused and seemed to be deciding how to answer the question, and finally said, "Naturally we do, as things can happen, and I need to make sure the investors' money is protected as much as it can be in this crazy business. So, in answer to your question, Dawna is heavily insured. I can't tell you to the exact penny how much, but it's a hefty amount.

"Hmm," thought Willis, *"I wonder if that's really the truth or is Gibson hiding something?"*

Gibson went on to say, "The truth is, If she were forced to leave the show because of this attacker, I'm not sure the insurance would cover that. In fact, I'm not sure how the show would survive, and that would be a great loss for me as I'm in this to win and win big! I want a show that runs for years and years and has numerous road shows, including productions in London and, hopefully, Japan. But I can't hope to move forward if I don't have a viable standby to cover for Dawna if Dawna were to die or become incapacitated. I would need to sign up a standby who the audience would want to see, and that isn't possible until we open and I have great reviews. I'm in a difficult position at the moment. God, I wish I could get Sutton Foster."

With that, Gibson excused himself, saying, "I'm sorry, but I have to get back to work. Find out who's attacking our show and star and when you do, I'll kill the son of a bitch!"

And so, as time moved on, Willis and Ross kept searching for the culprit while the show itself continued to improve. Soon the Boston run was over, and Gibson had the promise of an excellent show but a nervous star and cast.

Act 3, Scene 1
Broadway!

At the end of the Boston run, the actors had a much-needed break while the sets were struck, trucked to New York, set up, and relit in the Lunt-Fontanne Theatre at 205 West 46th Street in the heart of the theatre district. With its seating capacity of just over 1,500, it had housed such hits as *Hello, Dolly!* and *Beauty and the Beast* and was ideal for Gibson's show.

The load-in went smoothly as the crew was seasoned and knew their craft. However, it took a good ten days to complete the load-in, as the IATSE stagehands occasionally like to stretch out their work time. Gibson's office had arranged for a catering service to keep a table in the basement supplied with muffins, bagels, cream cheese, lox, plus an assortment of luncheon meats, large coffee urns with both regular and decaf, and one with hot water for tea. Keeping the crew well-fortified was just good business and Gibson's office knew how to keep things running smoothly in that area.

As the show settled into the theatre, the wardrobe got set up in the basement with the costumes for the various actors ironed, steamed, and placed in the appropriate dressing rooms. Another two-day technical rehearsal was called to set the final focus on the lighting and review the sound cues, etc., with the cast. It was a relief to most actors to have had the break and to now be in the home stretch in preparation for the opening night four weeks ahead. Preview ticket prices were the same as for the rest of the run of the show, so Gibson normally wouldn't have cared if the show, for whatever reason, had to be delayed but now he wanted it to open in time to qualify for this year's Tony Awards. He was heard to say, "Fingers crossed, I hope it's smooth sailing from now on." He could not have been more wrong.

Because of the disruptions in Boston, the cast and crew were less focused as they might have been, so having preview time before the opening was a blessing and very important.

It was now late March, and Willis and Ross were joined by their partner Monty, as he was on his spring break from Yale and was quickly brought up to date. It was a lot for him to absorb and there were still few leads to help solve the mystery of who was trying to hurt Dawna.

Meanwhile, Dawna's performance kept improving, but she still remained edgy and less than cooperative. In the new theater there was a problem with positioning the two greenrooms. There was plenty of room stage left but simply no room stage right. Peggy, being the ever-resourceful stage manager, discovered that outside of Dawna's dressing room was sort of a small anteroom that could house three or four chairs and a few small tables. *"Perfect,"* thought Peggy. *"I'll just check with Dawna to make sure she's ok for the actors to use that area as the other greenroom during the show."*

But when she approached Dawna, she was coolly told, "Fine, use it, but only for certain actors." News of that slight flew through the theatre like wildfire and suddenly everyone was, once again, less than sympathetic to their star.

Meanwhile, the actors went through the tedious tech rehearsal where the lighting was checked out and adjusted, sound cues worked into the action, props set up, quick wardrobe chances rehearsed and so forth. Fiona was at her lighting board in the back of the house along with a set-up for the audio technicians. Jens had a table set up about halfway back, near a production table for Gibson and Trish and their team. As Peggy guided the show through its first and then second act, Fiona lit the actors and scenes as the scenes progressed.

Once again Dawna stayed in her dressing room and one of the lesser actors was quickly assigned to stand in for her, but this time it was as though Dawna was trying to hide from her would-be attacker. "*The hell with the damned lighting,*" she thought. It's not that she hadn't learned her lesson about the importance of good lighting on her. She was simply scared… scared to death and was cowering away from whatever was out there that might harm her. It was a feeling that was totally new to Dawna, and it deeply alarmed and concerned her. she was used to being in total control of her life and that control was quickly slipping away.

Meanwhile, Gibson was furious at Dawna for not participating in the tech rehearsal. Her refusal was unheard of, but Gibson was helpless what with the potential treat of her walking off the show. This would be especially disastrous for Gibson financially, as he knew that if this show suddenly closed due to audiences wanting to see Dawna and only Dawna, he and Trish would most likely have to shut down their offices, which would in effect cause their world to totally collapse.

After two days of teching the show, Allison called for a full-dress rehearsal where the show would be run full out with an invited audience of friends and associates of the show. This typically would be an "up" performance, because the audience would be mostly made up of friends and cheerleaders of the cast and crew. It typically would be an exciting and fun time, and it was. The performance went on without a hitch except for two missed lighting cues and one mistimed sound cue.

Despite this and the wonderful theatricality of the show's closing moment, Allison had had it with dealing with Dawna. At best, she was high-strung and now was certifiably impossible. The show was "one unending nightmare" and he couldn't wait for it to open "so I can get as far away from this fucking show and that crazy cunt as possible!" He did, however, have to admit that when Dawna was lifted up on that pedestal in the closing, the effect was terrific and there was no doubt that she was "One hell of a star!".

Act 3, Scene 2
More Shows Within the Show Are Added

Meanwhile, there was an additional show taking place out in front of the theatre. Remembering the idea that Alex Cohen had used with Marlene Dietrich years ago, Gibson had included in the show's budget a fun and effective promotional stunt. He hired a dazzling white hardtop Rolls-Royce which was parked outside the stage door of the theatre. There was also a gleaming chrome ladder next to it and after each show, Gibson had Dawna go out the stage door, walk through a cordoned-off path to the Rolls through the adoring crowds. She would then climb up the ladder and sit on the roof of the car, autographing fans' programs. On evening performances there were also Klieg lights which sent up intense shafts of lights that could be seen from blocks away and that drew crowds.

including the audiences from other nearby shows as they let out. All very theatrical, very effective, and lucrative as Gibson somehow managed to keep the box office open so the onlookers could buy tickets to see Dawna's show.

This business worked like a charm on many levels. it raised people's awareness of the show and its star, helped build up the ticket sales, fed Dawna's ego and, strangely enough, enabled her to feel safe and appreciated. Her theory, while wildly flawed, was: "if someone wanted to harm me, it would have to be from an internal source… to date, no one outside the theatre has poses a threat to me." This clearly was totally crazy and lacking in logic, but Dawna was getting less and less rational as the pressures on her increased.

This gimmick worked great until Dawna, in her egomaniacal way, irritated Gibson to the breaking point. He had put up with having to hire painters to paint her dressing room not once but twice because "The first beige-y pink color was not exactly right for my skin tones." And after that, there were all sorts of unending demands. But what finally was the last straw was the issue of the dog. Gibson had gone and bought a Havanese as a surprise replacement for the one that had been poisoned. The dog came with a price tag of $3,500 that the show's budget could ill afford and was intended as a surprise gift for Dawna. The surprise ended up being that she all but threw the dog back at Gibson. "There's no pleasing that bitch! Not even with another expensive bitch!" he was heard to mutter.

And so that evening when Dawna waltzed out of the stage door, there were no klieg lights, no Rolls… just the chrome ladder with no place to climb to, which emphasized the missing tribute. Dawna didn't speak to Gibson for a week, to which he responded, "It's been the best week for me since we started this show!"

As the preview weeks progressed, Allison and the cast worked at fine-tuning the show, cutting pieces of dialogue that weren't working, adding new lines to heighten the humor and drama of the show and it continued to get better and better. On top of that, during the first week of previews, the second act had been enhanced by a superb dance number that Kevin, the company's choreographer had come up with. That little addition of just four handsome male dancers caused the budget to go up more than a cool quarter of a million dollars what with their salary, transportation, hotel rooms, rehearsal time, costumes, and so forth. The ever-resourceful Gibson was running out of investors and was unable to get Lilah to fork over the needed money.

Cornered and desperate for the money to open the show, Gibson secured some additional funds from a questionable source, Harry Carlone, who was rumored to be connected to the mafia. This put additional pressure on Gibson, as he wasn't at all that sure of the consequences if the show failed and what Carlone might do if he didn't get his money back with considerable interest. Gibson had always been a gambling man and this show was perhaps the biggest gamble of his life. But then he tended to somehow always end up on his feet. Time would tell.

The dance number was a satire of the big "Slaughter on 10th Avenue" number from the MGM movie Words and Music, a forgettable movie but one that contained a stunning dance number within it. Kevin had Dawna dance a pas de deux with Romain Rogers, one of the dancers in the chorus. Romain was tall, ruggedly handsome, strong, and very, very sexy. He clearly caught Dawna's eye as Clarrisa watched on enviously. The number was pulled together quickly and came off smoothly to everyone's amazement, to Gibson's delight and to Marshall's irritation.

In the number, Romain made Dawna look great as he was patient, strong, and the perfect partner for her. In the dance, there was a stylized fight scene where Dawna, at the end of the number, in a fit a jealousy shoots Romain and then looks back in great sadness and regret as the police leads her away from Romain's crumpled body. The audience loved it, and it gave the second act the punch it so clearly needed. It also was strangely prophetic.

Dawna was thrilled with the new number and eagerly submerged herself in learning the steps and action. It served several purposes: not only did it give the show the much-needed shot of energy into the rather slow second act, it gave Dawna a new focus and a distraction away from her troubles. She found Romain to be an excellent dancer and partner, strong and very masculine. She was suddenly wildly happy with learning the role and focused on trying hopefully to be as good as her partner. Luckily, he had been given the difficult parts of the dancing, but Kevin's choreography made Dawna look really good and that she was holding up her end in the number.

Romain also turned out to be a smart and very nice guy, and he and Dawna clearly hit it off from the very first moment when they started to learn the number. *"Strange."* she thought. *"He's been here in the show ever since the four men were added a while ago, but I never really noticed him. He certainly is handsome. Much too young for me but…"*

Jens came up with a simple but really eye-catching set mostly consisting of stylized props including a bar, several café tables and chairs, and a chandelier all in white… simple and affordable, much to Gibson's relief. Fiona, in turn, outdid herself with the lighting… It started with Dawna upstage, lit in silhouette on a platform leading into a bar and ended up with her being led away to jail, again in silhouette. In a way it was like a breath of fresh air after all that everyone had been through. It was fun and good for the show and especially satisfying for Dawna… almost an oasis in what had been a hard and tense time for her.

In the number, Dawna's and Romain's characters connect in a chance meeting in a bar. Dawna wanted to make sure she wasn't playing a hooker, which she was assured was not the case, but clearly that's exactly the part she was playing. They had a very hot pas de deux with the other male dancers eventually joining in, trying to gain Dawna's attention, but all her character saw was Romain as he took charge of her and beat away his competitors. It was a hot, sexy, fun number until the couple gets into a conflict and Dawna's character grabs a gun and shoots him. Why the conflict or where she got the gun defied logic, but who cared? The number made Dawna look extremely good and the audience loved it.

Tony's job was to find the furniture and, more importantly, a gun that looked menacing and of course the needed blanks. It was placed behind the edge of one of the show's wings and worked perfectly. Tony, as the prop master, was super cautious due to the Alec Baldwin incident in *Rust* when Baldwin took a prop gun that was accidentally loaded with real ammunition and killed the cinematographer on the movie. Tony would carefullly check the gun out at the beginning of each show and there it waited to be grabbed and fired at the end of the dance number. All went well the first three times the number was performed, and everyone was elated at the audience's reaction.

The number brought down the house, partially because no one realized that Dawna could really dance. The fact was she had never really been given the chance. Also, Kevin had shrewdly designed the number so that Romain did most of the work with the lifts, etc. while Dawna looked gorgeous in the simple but very effective costume that Elina had whipped up in a matter of moments. God knows how.

On the fourth night, there was an envelope addressed to Dawna in green ink on her dressing table that she somehow missed as her dressing table looked like an explosion in a shingle factory with papers, letters, and fan mail everywhere. The note said:

I BET YOU'D KILL FOR A HIT SHOW!

Everyone had started to relax in terms of worrying about whoever was writing those crazy notes with green ink as the show was taking everyone's attention and that last note, while not at first found, not only didn't sound threatening, it just didn't make sense.

That night Dawna and Romain did their dance number and at the end of the number, as rehearsed, she shot him, he crumpled and fell to the stage floor as Dawna's character was arrested. She was led away and a special curtain for the number came down to cover the scene. Dawna quickly ran around to stage left and came out in front of the curtain for the show within the show to thunderous applause, but she stood alone. The applause was deafening. They loved it but Romain didn't enter from stage right as he always did. Dawna bowed, took the applause, and was heard to mutter under her breath, "Where the hell is Romain?" He never came in from stage right and for a good reason: the prop gun had real bullets in it and Dawna had actually shot Romain. Fortunately, she was a better actress and dancer than a marksman.

The show came to a complete stop. Peggy came out front and made a brief announcement, saying, "There's been a slight technical problem, but we will resume the show shortly." The show re-commenced with a very shaken and confused cast. Romain was swiftly taken to a nearby hospital with what turned out to be a flesh wound and was released the next day. It looked like he and the number would be out of the show for maybe a week, as no one had understudied his part so he couldn't be replaced.

Consequently, there was no dance number and the show suffered because of it. However, the press caught wind of what had happened and had a field day and, wouldn't' you know it, the box office picked up even more. Tony, the propman, was promptly questioned by the police. He was even given a lie detector test and then released. Soon he quit the show and he and his wife left town two days later to live with their son in Lake Tahoe.

Monty, at Willis's suggestion, checked out Marshall and found out that his understudy had gone on for him that day, as Marshall had spent a good part of the day plus the evening in the hospital with all sorts of complaints. Midafternoon the doctors prescribed a neuropathic pain agent, which ended up being a totally wrong prescription for his problem. All the prescription did was increase Marshall's depression. With that, Carol came by the theatre to gather some of Marshall's belongings.

Later that week, Romain was able to return to the show and his duet with Dawna. A few of the lifts had to be modified, but the dance remained strong and continued to be a crowd pleaser. Once again, the show's cast was on tenterhooks knowing there was someone out there who wanted the show and its star to fail. It went without saying that now everyone was on the alert for any new notes with a green warning.

The next day, to Dawna's credit, she called Tony and said, "Hi is Tony Krasne there?"

To which Tony replied, "This is Tony. Who's calling?" knowing full well that it was Dawna Drake on the other end of the line as her voice was so distinctive, but not believing it really was her calling.

"Tony, this is Dawna Drake. I'm calling because I wanted to let you know that I understand your distress with what has happened with this show and why you have decided to leave. I don't blame you. If I were in your shoes, I'd leave too," she said with a little nervous laugh and followed with

"I want to thank you for all your help and support. I hope someday we'll work together again."

Tony gulped and managed to say, "Thank you very much Miss Drake. I'm sorry that I had to leave but the show was just so distressing… so upsetting."

There was a long pause and finally she said, "I will never forget what you did. In several ways you saved my life. Thank you." And she hung up.

Tony immediately called three of his friends on the show and told them about Dawna's call, and word about the call made the rounds on the fast track.

In a strange way, most of the cast began to sympathize with its star. It's hard enough when one is carrying the show as Dawna was doing, but to be vulnerable to a crazed assailant was hard to imagine. For her, the pressure had to be unbelievable and so the company in general started to give Dawna a little slack when it came to judging her. Maybe she wasn't all that bad. Dawna, when she got wind of Marshall and Trish's developing friendship, thought maybe she had been a bit too hard on Marshall and started to cozy up to him, which drove Trish more than a bit crazy.

Act 3, Scene 3
Another Theory...
Another Take

Later that week, Romain caught Ross as he was getting a cup of coffee down in the basement and said, "I know you guys have been investigating those green messages. Do you want my take on it?"

Willis had told Ross, "Hang around and chat with the cast. I think there's a lot we could learn from them."

So, Ross said to Romain, "Sure, let's grab a coffee and sit and chat." Ross noted that while it was clear that Romain was still suffering a bit from that flesh wound, he was young and very healthy and consequently was back in the show sooner than expected.

They found two chairs in a quiet corner of the basement. Romain, who was carrying a canned health drink, sat down and took a sip while Ross started on his coffee. With that, Ross asked Romain, "How are you feeling? I bet getting shot like that came as a big shock and must have been incredibly painful."

"Well, that's probably the understatement of the year," replied Romain. "But I have a bit of a secret: like most dancers, I have an ongoing bout with pain much of the time and what works for me is to take a Tylenol or the CVS equivalent, which is less expensive, along with an eyedropper of CBD oil—the non-hallucinatory type which cuts the pain down to about ten percent. That has enabled me to stay away from the heavier painkillers that were prescribed for me by the doctors. I'm very careful not to get hooked on any strong drugs."

He grinned, paused and then went on to say, "As to the subject at hand, it seems to me that the person who put the real bullets in the gun wasn't looking to kill me. He was trying to mess with Dawna's head… Make her freak out. What that person didn't realize was that by the time Dawna's character goes to shoot me, Dawna is wildly out of breath as the dance routine just before the gun bit is very strenuous for her and she's always shaking a bit. I'm amazed that she even winged me. That makes me think that the person who's responsible for the green messages was trying to totally unnerve Dawna."

"I wonder if Dawna's looking for a way to get out of the

show. I probably shouldn't tell you this, but she told me that one time early on, while we were just learning our number, that she was ready to quit the show. Apparently, there's a terrific TV series in the offering if she were to be free of *Mad About the Gal!* Now, she seems to be up on our show."

"Very changeable, that woman. Ah, I almost forgot, there's a bit of gossip going around that Marshall is having an affair with Trish. I have no idea if it's true, but it is an interesting bit of business, eh?" With that, Romain excused himself and left.

Ross found Romain's comments useful especially the information about Marshall's and Trish's possible affair, which was curious, VERY curious.

Back on stage, for the finale, Allison had asked that a scrim be added to the number. Its purpose was to add more theatrical mystery to the number. The scrim, a flat, gauze-like material, was just downstage in front of Dawna's elevator between it and the audience. With Fiona's lighting, it appeared to be a solid wall but as the elevator brought Dawna up to its full height, the lights on the front of the scrim would lower and Dawna's special lighting would come up so that the audience would see Dawna magically appear, floating upward and end up standing there, in her stunning red gown with her arms stretched out as if saying "Here I am!" All very effective!

A special electronic release would then free the scrim so

it would drop to the floor, be sucked into a hole in the stage floor and disappear out of sight while Kevin choreographed the dancers to move around the pedestal saluting Dawna, the star of the show!

Later it was also arranged to have a new, revolutionary effect called "Pyro Perfect" added to the finale. As Dawna made her appearance, "Pyro Perfect" would drop from above and fall down around Dawna and the stage. This was a combination of confetti and small firework-like explosions that was housed in a large wooden box above Dawna but out of sight of the audience. Its purpose was to celebrate Dawna's appearance and was extremely effective, so much so that it was decided to add the affect over the audience during the final curtain call to everyone's delight… and much to Gibson's chagrin. One more expense the show's budget could ill afford, but hey, Dawna was selling tickets, so fingers crossed that the opening would garner excellent reviews and the ticket sales that Gibson would need to keep the show open.

The look of Dawna standing on the platform in that spectacular red costume with her remarkable face made such a fantastic impression that Gibson followed Trish's suggestion and ordered a life-sized cutout, color photo blowup of the pose. It was that image that brought the audience to its feet at every performance, so having it in the lobby not only looked great, it acted as a tease to get people to want to see Dawna in the show. It quickly became a popular photo used in promoting the show much to Clarrisa's chagrin. Gibson's only regret was that he hadn't had its likeness when he made up the show poster.

Back on stage there was a huge discussion when Fiona insisted that she had to light Dawna on the pedestal and Allison was finally able to talk Dawna into coming out of her dressing room and stand on her platform for the final pose so she could be properly lit.

Later, Willis suggested to Ross that they talk to Allison after the show, and it was agreed that the best time would be to try to catch him at The nearby "Rendezvous" Bar early before he got too drunk. The two men said goodnight to the doorman, walked out of the theatre, and immediately were glad that it was a short walk as it had started to rain and neither had thought to carry an umbrella. They soon arrived at the bar and found Allison in one of the booths with its worn, fake leather banquette seats, nursing a scotch. He nodded to the two men and Willis asked, "Like some company?"

Allison, gesturing for the men to sit down said "Sure, why not?"

"So, how's it going?" Willis asked.

"It all depends on when you ask me," as he gestured to the waiter for him to refill his glass and said, without much enthusiasm, "What'll you two have?" To which Willis ordered a Pinot Grigio with a back of ice and Ross asked for "Just a Coke, please."

"Seriously, how's it going and what's your take on things in general?"

"Well, that's an interesting question as this show keeps shifting around as new problems pop up. I sometimes equate it to trying to nail Jello to the wall. Strange, in many ways it's not that difficult a show but as you can see, we've had our share of problems that are rather unique. I sure wish I knew who was testing Dawna with those notes. I'd like to thank him in person as I just love seeing that cunt cornered. I've worked with a lot of high-strung stars but she gets the prize for being the most egotistical, difficult bitch to date." He paused and then said, "But the bottom line is she does sell tickets and that's hard to ignore."

"Who do you think is upsetting her with those notes?" Ross asked.

Allison took a sip of his drink and then took his cocktail napkin and absentmindedly unfolded it and then refolded it as he thought. He finally said, "It could be any number of people, but if I were a betting man, I would say it's a woman. I have no evidence. It's just a hunch but I'll bet you twenty dollars that I'm right." Grinning, he added, "Of course there's just a 50-50 chance of my winning that bet."

"Sorry, Allison, I'm not a betting man." After a brief pause while Willis took a sip of his drink, he said, "Seriously, we need to find out who's sending those notes and we need to find out fast before someone gets hurt, namely Dawna. So, tell me of the females on our show, who do you think is capable of hurting Dawna?"

"Well, guys, that kinda puts me on the spot." He paused, stirred the ice in his drink, and finally said, "I think Clarrisa would get my vote. She is one tough, very smart lady and is extremely ambitious and, yes, jealous. Next time you see her on stage at the same time with Dawna, watch her. She exudes hatred and I'm not so sure she's acting. Clarrisa is the ultimate pro and has zero tolerance for unprepared actors. Did you ever notice Clarrisa's face when Dawna used to go up on her lines when we were in Boston? When it happened, Clarrisa was a show unto herself."

"Of course, there's also Elina to consider. I directed a show once called *Fabulous Flamenco* and the female star on that fiasco had a solo flamenco number which required her to have a long train of a skirt. You know the type with lots of ruffles, the type real Flamenco dancers know how to use. If used correctly their skirts almost become living scenery. Really wonderful and smashing. The star of that show, who will remain nameless until I have my third drink, rehearsed in a skirt made of muslin so she could get used to working it throughout her number. Well, after two weeks of practicing with that damned skirt, the time came to use the real one as we got ready to do a dress run-through. I'm not sure why, but the lady in question could not make that skirt work and finally Elina just grabbed a pair of the largest pair of scissors I've ever seen from her assistant and hacked off the train to that dress. It ruined the dress and the number was ultimately cut, but I'd pay admission to see Elina in action like that again. She was magnificent! I love people who don't take crap from anyone."

"I would also keep an eye on Peggy. She's one tough cookie. That's why I asked for her. She's smart, clever, and extremely dedicated and it's kind of fun to watch Dawna piss her off... a dangerous thing to do, mind you. I've seen Peggy reduce strong ladies to tears when they didn't listen to Peggy's directions. It rarely happens as most actors are totally aware that Peggy knows her way around a theatre. She's one tough broad."

To which Willis said, "Talk about tough, you're about as tough as they come. If I may be so bold, I'd like to say you are one hard, sarcastic guy." Allison just smiled, as he clearly agreed with Willis's appraisal. "How did you get that way?" asked Willis.

Allison sort of scratched the stubble on his chin and said, "Ha, you can thank my father for that. He was one son of a bitch. He was always criticizing me and goading me on. So out of defense I became very sarcastic, and I mean VERY! He once announced sarcastically in front of our family and friends that I, his son, was an accident. My reaction was (being a typical kid at that age), I opened my wallet, took out a condom which we all carried but seldom got a chance to use, and tossed it at him and said, 'Next time keep that pecker of yours under wraps!' He never crossed me after that. Hey, if I could keep that bastard cowed by a bit of sarcasm, it was a talent worth nurturing. I will say that in some sort of sick way I loved my father, I just didn't like him." He looked at his watch and said, "Well, it's getting late and I have another full day tomorrow. I wish you guys luck. You have one hell of a job ahead of you. Makes my work look like a piece of cake."

Allison then took a final gulp of his drink, gestured towards Willis's and Ross's drinks as he yelled over to the bartender, "Put these on my tab" and he was gone.

And so, the show moved forward. Gibson and Allison revved up their efforts to tighten up the show, as it was running a bit long, while Gibson and Trish worked hard to keep their star as well as the cast and crew happy. One Saturday evening after the show, they gave a party as a means of thanking everyone for hanging in there. While everyone seemed to appreciate the gesture, there was a lack of unity in the cast. Most seemed to be occupied and worrying about the upcoming opening and what might happen next with the green messages."

Gibson, being nobody's fool, took advantage of the mystery attacks by leaking stories to the press about the threats.

Gibson came up with a name and told the press that the cast was calling it "The Green Death." People who wanted to see the show often had to rely on getting their seats from scalpers, often paying double the ticket price, a sure sign that there was a hit in the works. The public was eating up the "Green Death" and the show ticket sales were soaring through the roof. Both Gibson and Trish were delighted, but expressed great concern for Dawna's safety while Willis, Ross, along with Monty when he was free, worked tirelessly to get to the bottom of this nightmare.

Trish tried constantly to comfort Dawna, and was often seen in her dressing room or watching her performance both from out front and from the wings. Since Dawna needed a confidante, she gravitated towards Trish and Trish comforted Dawna as best she could, but urged her to be extra careful and alert. In a curious way, Trish's admonitions made Dawna even more nervous.

The next afternoon, Willis sat down with Ross and Monty, and each grabbed a coffee from the craft services table in the basement. Monty and Ross each had decaf and Willis had a regular. Willis took some salad and the brothers each grabbed a doughnut. Willis frowned at the two young men and commented that he wished that they would eat healthier, to which both said in unison, "Yeah, Dad," and everyone laughed.

And so, they began to review the cast for a potential

murderer. "Let's go down the list and see if there is anything we've missed." Willis said. "At the top, just in terms of billing, etc. is Dawna. My gut feeling is that she would do almost anything at this point not to jeopardize the show. In truth, anything is possible with these crazy egomaniacs. Of course, she had no way of knowing that Tony would catch the fact that the prop coffee wasn't what it was supposed to be, but I suppose just that once she could have ducked when the coffee was thrown. But she didn't, so I have my doubts about her being the culprit here."

"I've been keeping my eye on Gibson. He's unusually crafty at promoting his show and star, but he's deeply in debt. I'm not so sure about Trish, his wife. Something is a bit off with that woman. Ever notice how she fingers that string of pearls she always wears when she's nervous? How about you conducting a bit of research on her, Monty?" Monty nodded his agreement.

"Next, let's look at Marshall Ward. As her leading man, he ought to be totally behind the show and its star, but you'd have to be blind not to see how difficult Dawna has been to him. The problem is: the threats against Dawna apparently started before their affair began to sour. Also, he was off the show and in the hospital when the real ammo was put in the gun, so it's likely that he's not our culprit but have we been blind to something here?"

Both Ross and Monty shrugged, as neither had a clue.

"Now, Clarrisa is a prime candidate for the would-be murderer. She clearly hates Dawna with every bone in her body and has access to all areas backstage, but if she were to kill off Dawna it would be the end of the show and her chances for any recognition, and we know these actors live for that! That said, let's keep a careful eye on her. Ross, see if you can dig up any dirt on her that might shed some light on the situation and be of any help to us."

At that, Willis added: "There are two characters in this story that I've been looking at but can't see any reason for them to be a villain in the piece. First, there's Lilah. We all know she's capable of a great many evil things… hell, Monty, she tried to kill you and your father, but in this case it just wouldn't make sense. She's heavily invested financially and emotionally in the show being a success and killing off its star just doesn't add up. Also, from all indications they are the best of friends."

The other person is Nat: sure, she could have taken a small amount of the poisoned candy, just enough to get sick but not die and in the process to throw us off, but I'm not so sure. The fact that she's been around the show would make it reasonably easy for her to substitute acid for prop coffee and to put real bullets into that gun. Any ideas here?"

To which the brothers again shook their heads and said "Nope" at the same time.

"Now, Allison Duprey is a guy to keep an eye on. We

all know he can be mean as the devil, vindictive, and just downright evil, but losing his star wouldn't help him one bit. No, I'd love to pin all this on him, but I suspect in this case he has Teflon skin and none of our suspicions or speculations would stick."

"As for the creative team, I doubt that Jens would want to scuttle the show, but then Dawna has been campaigning to eliminate his wonderful a vista set change at the end of the first act. You know Dawna is used to getting her way. You and I wouldn't think that was a strong enough motive to hurt someone but who knows in this crazy business. The lure of getting a Tony award might be incentive enough, but then no Dawna could easily equate to no show and no chance of a Tony."

"The same for Elina. We all know what a bitch Dawna has been and how she has sabotaged some of Elina's' creative efforts. I personally saw Elina's reaction when Dawna made that entrancea while ago in an outfit she bought on her own at Bergdorf Goodman's and wore at the beginning of the second act. Gibson showed me the bill she gave him for that outfit. Hard to imagine a little ensemble running into five figures. I could see Elina getting even, but severely injuring her… Who knows?"

"As for Fiona, while we know that Dawna has been less than cooperative when it's comes to the tech rehearsals, it's hard to think it would cause a person to scuttle a production over that. In that area, Dawna is her own worst ene-my and when it comes to lighting, she's doing herself more harm than anyone else."

"There is no way that our choreographer Kevin Travis could be involved, as he came onto the scene after the threats had been around for a while. The same is true for Romain, as the male dancers were added after the appearance of the poisoned candy. Also, I doubt that Romain would run the risk of testing Dawna's marksmanship ability," he said with a grin.

"I'm not sure about Felix Rudder, the fight captain. I can't see a motivation on his part but then anyone who likes a good fight might get swept up with the idea of nailing a bitch of a star. Any thoughts on this?" To which Ross said, "Actually I checked out his schedule and on the day when the real bullet was put into the gun he was out of town prepping a movie shoot. So, my guess is it's a dead-end, pardon the bad pun."

"Got it, Ross," Willis said with a chuckle. Then going down his list, he said, "I think we can eliminate Dale Goodwin, Dawna's agent, not because they've at times been close and at other times been at great odds with each other, but my research shows that Dale, like Felix, has been out of town during much of this fracas."

"Now Roz, who is head of wardrobe on the show has a big ax to grind. Our star has been putting Roz through hell on a regular basis. Did you know that as a result, Roz has been secretly and quietly taking in Dawna's costumes a tiny bit at a time every few days, so Dawna is being driven crazy thinking she's gaining weight? Don't ask me how I know… I just know. And while it's kind of funny thinking about it, it most likely isn't an action that would indicate that it was a precursor to murdering someone. I just don't know. We're missing something here and at the moment I can't put my finger on it."

To add the stress, there was a potential stagehand strike that, if it occurred, would stop the show cold, but that wouldn't happen for a good two months and there was plenty to worry about now, so that concern was temporarily tabled.

As if there wasn't enough drama around, one day Dawna walked into her dressing room and found a young guy, maybe 16 or 17, in her dressing room just looking around and touching her costumes. When Dawna demanded "Who the fuck are you and what the hell are you doing in my dressing room?" Being the actress she was, she projected as much authority and alarm into her voice as she could and with an abundance of volume to match. The young man panicked, said "I… I was just looking…" And tore out of the room, down the hall and out the stage door. Upon investigating, it turned out that Hal, the usual stage doorman, was on his lunch break and the person assigned to cover for him believed the kid when he said "I have an envelope to deliver to Miss Drake. Can you tell me where Miss Drake's dressing room is?" Dawna, in near hysterics, was finally placated when Gibson said he would hire a cop to keep an eye on Dawna and her dressing room. This time it would be a real cop, actually one who was moonlighting and happy to make the extra money.

The only issue was Dawna found the policeman to be a bit more attentive when she was in her dressing room, so it was agreed that when she needed to use it, he would do a thorough sweep of the space to make sure that no one had gotten into it while Dawna was on stage or out and then he was to wait outside her door to make sure no one got to her.

Act 3, Scene 4
Opening Night

Suddenly opening night arrived. The show was rock solid with the audiences loving it and the show was already sold out for the next half year. It looked like everyone was in for a long, satisfying run. Even Allison seemed pleased. The one exception was Marshall Ward, who was not particularly happy as his part had been cut down to practically nothing and he was stuck with a two-year contract. His love scenes with Dawna had become a real test of his acting ability despite Dawna trying to make nice with him. Trish had warned him to "Be very careful with that bitch."

Clarrisa, too, was not happy, as there was a very good possibility that Dawna might just once again beat her out when Tony time came around. She thought, *"Maybe I should have taken supporting actress billing,"* as she certainly would win a Tony that way, but her ego would never have let her take that billing, *"…and let Dawna have the satisfaction."*

When it came around to Allison, Jens, Elina, and Fiona, all four were clearly in the running in their various categories. And Gibson, along with Trish, was feeling optimistic that the show would be the hit that they needed. It really was a case of if the show failed, Gibson would most likely have to close his offices and, possibly worse yet, face Harry Carlone who was not used to losing and had a reputation for "getting even" with anyone who, as he would say "Didn't deliver da goods." Interestingly enough, Gibson was the eternal optimist in that he somehow always ended up winning. Trish, on the other hand, seemed to be cracking under the stress. She seemed less focused and appeared erratic at times.

Gibson noticed it first, then Marshall and soon after, Willis. The pressure on everyone was beginning to tell in different ways. On everyone's mind was the question: who is the one who's been trying to attack Dawna? First, she had almost been poisoned, then almost disfigured by acid, and then the loaded gun that did a good job of almost undermining her confidence, except she had an ego that seemed impregnable. She could get thrown and upset, but ultimately it seemed that nothing could permanently penetrate her confidence. So, it was hard to tell if everyone's nerves were keyed up for the opening or just plain raw from apprehension about "The Green Death." Probably a bit of both.

Now the previews were over, and the show was as good as it would ever get. It was the home stretch, and everyone had his or her fingers crossed that the onslaught of disasters aimed at Dawna would finally be a thing of the past and everyone could hopefully settle into a long, enjoyable, and profitable run. Questionable logic at best.

The morning of opening night started off easy enough. There were the usual flowers and yes, people now sent texts in lieu of telegrams wishing everyone "Good luck", "A great show" and "Here's to a long run", etc. Thank God there were no notes with green lettering. Allison wanted to keep everyone revved up, so he broke tradition and gave some notes partially to keep everyone busy but also focused. He didn't really want to instigate any major changes, but he was always polishing a show and making every aspect as good as possible.

He just couldn't help it… a little change here and a little addition there. His theory was if he kept everyone's mind on the show, no one would mentally drift off or lose the keyed-up energy that made for a winning opening night. Allison knew that several key critics had already come before the opening and had undoubtedly written their reviews, but all he could do was keep the pressure on and pray. Luckily, the cast had a good feeling about the show and the last two performances had been as close to perfection as possible. Dawna, in particular, had been turning in a remarkable performance and was like a thoroughbred headed for the backstretch. She was out to win and nothing or no one was going to stop her!

Allison made the cast go through the finale number three times mostly to keep everyone busy and focused. Not so with Gibson and Trish. Gibson was occupied pushing for as much last-minute publicity as possible. Even though Gibson would usually use one of the assistants in the office, in an attempt to keep Lilah busy and to make her feel important, he gave her a list of people that he wanted to make sure were coming to see the show and would be at the party at Sardi's after the curtain came down.

He also called his PR people to make sure there was lots of coverage in the works. He wanted to make sure *People* magazine plus hopefully *Vanity Fair* would be there. He toyed with the idea of having the white Rolls Royce parked out front but instinctively knew Dawna would be beyond playing that scene at that point. She would want even more attention. Gibson did, however, make sure that the Klieg lights would be ablaze as the audience left the theatre.

Trish was kept busy dealing with those details that Gibson didn't have the time to take on, but focused she wasn't. There was a mix-up on some tickets that were to be set aside for some VIPs who Gibson was wooing, possibly for their next production. There were also notes to the cast to double-check and then arrange for them to be either placed in the cast's mailboxes backstage and, in some cases, along with gifts that were to be delivered to the more important cast members' dressing rooms. Trish had a small team of people from the office to help her.

While the cast and crew each got a jacket with a photo of Dawna in her final pose in that spectacular red dress on the back of the jacket, some of the jackets delivered ended up being the wrong size and it took some time for an assistant to rectify the screwup. While most of the cast disliked Dawna, at this point she visually represented the show and the show smelled like it was going to be a big hit. Consequently, almost everyone was thrilled to wear that image. Only Clarrisa and Marshall made a point of trashing their jackets, Marshall by giving it to his housekeeper and Clarrisa by taking a special pleasure in shoving it down her apartment incinerator chute.

Arranging for the distributing of the gifts with the appropriate notes was a bit too much for Trish, and as hard as she tried to work everything out, she got confused, which was very unlike her. To be fair, she had a lot on her plate, but she just wasn't her usual focused self. As an excuse for her confusion, she said that she was deeply concerned that Gibson had actually used a mafia connection to finance the last costs of the show and that was dangerous. In short, the future of Gibson's and her company had been hanging by a thread; it was imperative that they have a hit show to survive. She had tried to be attentive to Dawna, even if in Trish's mind she thought Dawna deserved all the stress she was under. As for Marshall, he was a dear, and while she had not meant for things to go as far as they had, she had to admit he had made great improvements in his lovemaking from when they were younger. In any case, she was determined that this opening would be one that no one would forget if only she could stay focused!

Clarrisa was strangely quiet when she arrived at the theatre… very low keyed. Clearly, she felt that while she was doing an excellent job in the show, she felt like a secondary character. Dawna was getting all the attention, especially with that damned jacket and Clarrisa didn't like that one bit so she proceeded to take out a bottle of green ink which she had recently purchased, and with some stationery started to print up a note, this time with a direct threat that Dawna was not going to survive the opening that evening.

As she was hiding the green ink and pen and deciding how and where to plant the note, she spotted a bottle of champagne on her dressing table with a card that had Dawna's name on it. Knowing that it had been sent to the wrong star of the show, she contemplated just chucking it into the wastebasket, but then thought *"Oh, what the hell"* and she went next door to Dawna's dressing room and said, "Someone left this in my room by mistake." Dawna, without really thinking, muttered "Thanks" and Clarrisa thought to say, "You're welcome, bitch" but reluctantly left off the word "bitch" and in the process almost forgot to include the note that came with the champagne on Dawna's dressing table. After Clarrisa left, Dawna took the bottle and out of curiosity opened the card and dammit, the note had green block letters that said:

DAWNA, YOU MADE IT THIS FAR.
IF YOU LIVE THROUGH THE FINALE TONIGHT
(AND I SERIOUSLY DOUBT YOU WILL)
I PROMISE YOU WILL NEVER
HEAR FROM ME AGAIN.

For the first time ever that anyone could remember, Dawna totally lost it. The pressure of opening night was hard enough on her, but this last note pushed her over the edge. Nat came into Dawna's dressing room to find Dawna swinging the bottle of champagne madly around the room hitting everything and anything in sight, but as hard as she swung it, the damned bottle refused to break. It was Dawna's spirit or the bottle that had to break and it looked like the bottle was winning.

Nat couldn't believe her eyes. She had never seen Dawna so out of control. Nat immediately ran and tried to find Allison. He was nowhere to be found until Harry, the stage doorman, upon hearing Nat calling out "Allison," quickly told her to check the Rendezvous Bar down the street from the theatre. "I think he was headed over there." Nat tore out the stage door, cut through the line of people trying to buy future tickets to the show, and rushed down the street and into the bar.

The lighting was low and it took a few moments for her eyes to adjust, but she finally found him in a dark corner of the bar, hunched over, glass in hand. She briefly wondered how many drinks he was into. She threw caution to the wind, grabbed him and swung him around on his stool and screamed, "You gotta come back to the theatre and get to Dawna's dressing room. She's hysterical! I've never seen her like this. I have no idea how she'll be able to perform tonight!"

It took Allison a moment to focus on Nat and what she was saying, but shortly he nodded his head, sighed, and got off his stool and took a last gulp of his drink before tossing some bills on the bar, then reluctantly followed Nat out the door. They pushed their way through the crowds on the ticket line and entered the stage door, made a mad dash to Dawna's dressing room where they could hear things crashing before they even entered through the opened door.

Allison stared at amazement as Dawna stood there panting, out of breath, with the champagne bottle still intact. One could see that her dressing room was practically destroyed. Opening night flowers were scattered everywhere, furniture was tipped over, the big dressing room mirror was smashed beyond belief, as were some of the lightbulbs that had surrounded it. Of her wardrobe, the special dress that was to be destroyed by coffee had been ripped to shreds. Luckily, it was the only costume that had suffered from Dawna's wild fury and there were the backup copies of it. Allison grabbed her, and to Nat's horror, he hauled off and slapped her across the face, and slapped her hard! Later it was discussed if he did it to snap her out of it or just used the occasion to do what he had wanted to do for days.

Nat quickly righted a chair and Dawna collapsed on it in sobs. Dawna eventually calmed down a bit, and as Willis and Ross arrived, Allison was finally able to find out exactly what was going on… or at least what Dawna thought might be going on. Clearly the person responsible for the green messages was planning one last attack. The threatening note was clear… Dawna was going to die, and no one yet had a clue as to who the perpetrator could be except Willis, who by now had a strong idea who had set this whole intense scene into action.

With very little time, Willis and Ross got Peggy and the new head propman together and told them he had a plan and he needed their help. He then pulled Kevin aside and told him his ideas, and in turn Kevin told Dawna what she needed to do. As Kevin explained what Willis expected of her, Dawna's crying started up again and Kevin worried about how well she understood what had to be done. Willis felt strongly that if Dawna balked at his suggestion, that tonight could easily be her last performance EVER!

Dawna eventually redid her makeup, changed into her opening costume, and steeled herself for the night ahead. This would have to be the performance of her life and she wasn't sure she was up for it.

Act 3, Scene 5
Crazy!

By 8:10 PM the audience was fully seated and there was a special buzz in the room. The cast was in its place and the all-important New York Times reviewer Sean Grayson was reportedly in the aisle seat he always took when reviewing Broadway shows. The overture began, and the lights dimmed in the theatre as the lights on the show drop went from a dull rosy color to a hot pink.

As the overture continued through the many familiar tunes, the drop changed colors thanks to Fiona's clever and sensitive lighting. There were also projections on the drop from time to time. As the audience greeted the end of the overture with an enthusiastic round of applause, the show curtain suddenly became transparent and one could see through it, the actors' home appeared, the show curtain flew out of sight and the show began!

The show clipped along, as Allison was especially good at pacing the action and his actors. The laughs came often and where they were supposed to be, and the concern for how the characters in the show were going to save the actors' home played remarkably well. The music helped to punch up the humor and pathos of the first act and Clarrisa's throwing of the coffee on Dawna had the best audience reaction ever. They loved seeing Dawna's character knocked down more than just a notch. Again, that single tear rolled down Dawna's cheek and one wondered if she was acting or just overwhelmed and might totally lose her composure.

The big worry now was, would the second act hold up and be as good as or better than Act One, and everyone was soon to find out. The comedy and pathos continued to play extremely well. Cora Williams at the elegant piano singing "La Vie en Rose" was extremely effective and when Clarrisa stood down stage center in her silver gown with thousands of rhinestones, she nailed "What'll I Do?" and the audience went wild with thunderous applause. But the dance number between Dawna and Romain topped everything and received a standing ovation.

Dawna was clearly touched and the cast, knowing how difficult it had been for her, applauded her from the wings. It was one of those rare, magical moments for the show, a moment that everyone had hoped for but had eluded them up to now. Everyone was riding high on the show, pulling together, and loving it!

And finally, the cast was in the home stretch. The actors had performed their individual numbers, all the scenes had gone exceptionally well, and now they attacked the big finale in the ballroom with new vigor. The dance number built until everyone in the cast looked upstage, extended their hands and voices as Fiona's lighting revealed Dawna's image through the scrim standing on an elevator as it slowly rose.

There she was first in silhouette then as the lights came up on her she stood there embracing the world to wild applause when suddenly the huge four foot by four foot by eight-foot wooden box that held the Pyro Perfect effect which was directly overhead and high above Dawna, appeared to have broken loose and crashed down onto Dawna. With her arms outstretched, it looked in a bizarre way it that she was welcoming this object. The audience and the cast were shocked. A number of ladies both in the audience and on stage screamed followed by an eerie silence.

And then the strangest thing happened: Dawna came out from the wings in her fantastic red dress, arms outstretched, and singing full out. The cast was at first stunned, having thought that they had just seen their star killed. But she was alive! Slowly and a bit hesitantly the cast and the band joined in for the last two stanzas of the finale. The finale came to its end with all the actors singing out in full voice, celebrating the success of the benefit and the conclusion of what was a wonderful, miraculous show. There were many pairs of eyes that were wet with tears.

The cast then took their curtain calls as Allison had directed: first, the secondary players, then the actors who played the more important characters with the audience cheering them on. Then Marshall came out of the wings to a nice round of applause, followed by Clarrisa who took her bow to wild applause, only to be topped when Dawna walked on to the stage and the audience was on its feet, cheering wildly. The ovation for Dawna was beyond what most in the audience had ever seen or heard. It lasted over five minutes nonstop as the cast joined in. The audience just refused to stop applauding. It was one of those truly unforgettable moments in theatre. Amazing! During Dawna's standing ovation, Gibson came on stage with Trish as they joined in the applause. Trish seemed distracted and confused.

After the curtain finally came down, Willis—to everyone's surprise—came on stage along with several uniformed policemen, who proceeded to cuff Trish as Gibson objected. The stunned cast looked on, including Dawna and Gibson, with everyone shouting questions. Willis raised his hands, motioning for everyone to quiet down, and when they finally settled down, he preceded to explain:

"As you all know, there have been a number of dire

threats directed to our star Dawna Drake via some notes in green ink. As hired investigators, Ross and I, along with some help from our partner Monty, reviewed our list of suspects and by a process of elimination, we suspected that Trish was the author of the green notes. We had eliminated her husband Gibson as he had too much to lose, as did Allison. For a while we seriously considered Clarrisa as the would-be murderer of Dawna, especially when we found some green ink hidden in her dressing room. Along with the ink were some sad attempts at creating threatening notes but the letter style was way off from the original threatening notes and, when confronted with these notes, Clarrisa confessed to just wanting to have 'A little fun and scare the hell out of Dawna'—which might have been very effective but not very productive in terms of keeping us on track towards nailing the culprit."

"As for the rest of the creative team including Jens, Elina, and Fiona, they were one hundred percent behind the show and its star even though personally they might not have been her biggest fans. As for the others such as Tad Morley the musical director, Lenny Leith the lyricist, Lilah, Nat, and even Marshall, all these suspects were not around when some of the attempts were made on Dawna's life… so that pretty much left just Trish. Of course, we weren't sure how and when she was going to attack Dawna. However, her last note indicated that Dawna would be attacked tonight and the word 'finale' in the note tipped me off as to when. Scratching his chin thoughtfully, Willis said, "I felt in my bones that it would have to be something spectacular. Thanks to our investigating Trish's past, we knew that she had a background in theatrical stagecraft, including rigging, before she moved on to producing. While I'll admit I wasn't 100 percent sure as to what she had in mind, I felt that it would be something highly theatrical. What better time to kill our star than at the very end of the opening night show?"

"So, I had our propman secretly take the life-sized cut-out profile of Dawna from the lobby and place it on the elevator platform in the basement. As you know, there are TV monitors strategically placed around the backstage area including one up in the fly loft where scenery is raised and lowered. When the profile of Dawna came up on the elevator behind the scrim and was lit up, it was impossible not to think it was the real Dawna. Both Peggy and Dawna had been tipped off by Ross and myself, so it really was a bit of staging that was comparatively easy to pull off. The box that fell down on Dawna's profile was a box that held the Pyro Perfect fireworks confetti which was to be used during the finale. Prior to the show, Trish, who we knew had a background in theatrical rigging, had been able to go up to the upper fly gallery and figure out how to release the lines that held the box high above the location where

Dawna would be standing in the finale, then later, when Trish saw Dawna (actually the profile of her) on the monitor come up on the elevator, she released the box so it would fall and kill our star."

"However, she wasn't aware that the image she saw was actually the promotional cutout profile of Dawna set out on the elevator as a stand-in for Dawna. I had prearranged to have Ross hide up in the fly gallery. As Trish released the box so it would fall and kill Dawna below, Ross took a video of her untying the rope as evidence and called me on my cell to let me know that we had her on video. Trish then raced down to enjoy her big moment, but it wasn't what she had expected, was it Trish?" asked Willis as he stared at her. "And so, ladies and gentlemen, there's a dramatic end that I bet you'll never forget!"

Trish, having been cuffed, was read her Miranda warning where the police advised her of her right to remain silent and, in effect, protect her from self-incrimination. However, before she was led out of the theatre, placed in one of the patrol cars, and taken to the city jail (shades of Dawna at the end of her dance number), Trish compulsively went on to confess that she had started off with the green lettered notes just for the fun of "scaring the hell out of Dawna," as she hated her for a number of reasons. When Gibson put a hand on her shoulder to stop, she brushed him off and went on to say, "Years ago I was dating an actor named Kent Lawrence. Dawna knew he and I were talking of getting married, and my take is Dawna couldn't stand to see two people happy when she was her usual miserable self, so she went after Kent. What she didn't know was that I had become pregnant, and I planned to have the child. But Dawna lured Kent away from me and he ended up breaking off our engagement. In desperation, I had an abortion which went badly, and as a result I've never been able to get pregnant again."

Choking back a sob, Trish said, "She killed my chances of ever having a child of my own. You didn't know that, did you, Gibson? So, Dawna, after playing with Kent for three or four months, got tired of the game and dumped him. God, I hated her then and even more so now. It was after that I had kind of an affair with Marshall who was so sweet and understanding… so comforting. But ultimately that didn't lead anywhere. Sometime later I met Gibson and ended up marrying him."

There was a pause, and finally Trish went on to say, "Where was I? I get so confused… Oh yes, I was against Gibson hiring Dawna as the star of *Mad about the Gal!* but he wouldn't listen to me, and so my hatred for her just grew and grew. At first it was kind of a game of "Let's mess with Dawna's head." I just loved her reaction to the green and purple fake flowers and the first note. Later, I was surprised that it was Nat who ended up in the hospital instead of

Dawna and oh, I was very upset about that poor little dog dying. I don't know, the game suddenly got more and more serious, and I got carried away with it. I just couldn't stop."

At this point Trish giggled. "I must say I enjoyed the reaction of Marshall to the note I sent to his wife Carol, as I had plans for Marshall and Carol to separate and for Marshall and myself to revisit old times. As for Dawna, she trusted me…. The stupid bitch!" she said, with a harsh smirk on her face. There was a pause and then she continued, "I despised her so much and it felt really good when attacking her."

As she said this, she nervously fingered her pearl necklace and suddenly it broke and sent pearls scattering in all directions. Strangely, the pearls echoed Trish's thoughts as the more she talked, the more scattered her logic became. Something that she didn't seem to comprehend was that if the pearls had in fact been really valuable, they would have been knotted in such a way that they would not come apart and scatter as they did. It was not clear if Gibson knew the pearls weren't the real deal or not either.

She went on to say, "As to when Dawna shot her dance partner Romain, I kinda liked the idea of messing with her mind… my wish was to….. completely destroy her, one way or another. I think that Dawna's so evil and should die or at the very least become so mentally unstable as to never be able to act again." She giggled at this thought. "I don't know. It's all got so sort of crazy and confusing, eh?" she asked of no one in particular. "In the end I didn't want to just scare Dawna, I wanted her dead. I almost did it, didn't I?" She said with a diabolical grin and then started to laugh and somehow couldn't stop.

One could still hear her hysterical laughter as she was put into a nearby police car and driven away. She was then interrogated and jailed until Gibson had his lawyers get her out, compliments of a hefty loan from his bank to pay her bail. This took longer than expected, but then this wasn't a movie made for television or a Jackie Collins novel. It took time to get things done.

Trish was diagnosed as mad…a psychopath; and while she was free on bail for a while, and never was sent to jail, she was eventually sent away to a mental institution. *Mad About the Gal!* was a huge success, and it looks like it will run profitably for a number of years with several touring companies as well as foreign productions. The show won a Tony award for Gibson and his partners, which gave his company the financial support it dearly needed.

Jens, Willis, and Fiona also each won a coveted Tony award, but Marshall wasn't even nominated. Dawna and Clarrisa were both nominated but they tended to cancel each other out so neither one won. Clarrisa, having not expected to win, took a certain delight in knowing that she had been the cause of Dawna's losing.

The show eventually made huge profits. Gibson quickly paid off Harry Carlone with considerable relief. It turned out that Carlone didn't understand the logistics of making a profit from a theatrical endeavor. All he saw was a series of hit reviews and long lines at the box office and he wanted his money back with a sizable markup and he wanted it immediately!

While it normally takes time before a show is in the black, after some not-so-subtle pressure on Carlone's part, Gibson was convinced that he'd best get the money owed to Carlone and get it to him FAST! Carlone and his people weren't in the habit of playing games and were not inclined to be patient. Luckily, Gibson was able to access the money needed out of the future ticket sales account by some clever bookkeeping on the part of his office manager.

As the show settled in for its long run, Gibson took some money out of the weekly profits for running his office and for paying himself his producer's fee, which was contractually considered part of the show's operating costs. Some of this income went towards securing Gibson's production company for future shows and also for paying for Trish's care at an expensive mental institute. Trish was institutionalized for two years before eventually being released. Kind of a short period considering, but not as short as the time it took Gibson to terminate their marriage.

And Dawna, after an excellent run-of-her-contract,

turned to doing a television series called "Dawna Knows," which many thought was a fabulous misnomer. As for TV, Dawna said "It's easier, much safer and much more profitable… Love those residuals!" Clarrisa took over Dawna's part as the lead and received a fee that was her best to date. Better than that, she starred in the London production, won an Olivier award, and sent a framed photo of herself receiving it to Dawna with the following note in green ink:

Dear Dawna,

I want to thank you for selling out to television. I have a question:

I hear that Meryl Streep has been signed to play your role of Lois Rae in the upcoming movie of our show *Mad about the Gal!* now apparently retitled *As Mad As They Get!* Is that true? I bet they don't get madder than you did when you heard that Meryl got your part.

LOL,

Clarrisa

Lilah promptly invested most of her winnings into a new musical called *Easy Come, Easy Go*. The title turned out to be prophetic, as most of her profits from *Mad About the Gal!* were quickly lost when her new show was a colossal flop and made the "wall of losers" at Joe Allen's.

Marshall ended up returning to television as the major star in a hit evening soap opera called "Grosse Pointe" and, as several people said, he found his true niche, career-wise.

Willis, Ross, and Monty soon started to solve two other mysteries: one which took place on a Yacht in Monte Carlo followed by a case involving a Continuing Care facility named Sunningdale.

Epilogue
The New York Times Review

Dawna Drake Gives an Arresting Performance

By Sean Grayson

Last night, during the finale of the new musical "Mad about the Gal!", the opening night audience got the most remarkable show within the show when during the finale, as she was performing her final number, we saw one of Broadway's most beloved performers, Dawna Drake, killed. A piece of scenery fell from above and appeared to have totally crushed her. It was the most upsetting, frightening moment I've ever experienced in all my days of going to the theatre. We, the audience were convinced that we had just witness the death of a great actress.

As it turned out, the falling piece of scenery hit an image of Dawna Drake but not Miss Drake. God, it was so real, so truly scary but luckily it was just an attempt to kill the star. You don't see that every day!

Now for the really good part: it turns out that the folks hired to protect Miss Drake, an organization called "The 3 in 1 Investigation Agency," had shrewdly tricked the would-be killer into thinking she was dropping a huge piece of scenery on Miss Drake. We, the audience, thought we had seen Miss Drake killed too, but seconds after her supposed death, out came our star singing the rest of the closing number! It was one of those magical moments on stage, one I'll never forget.

After the curtain calls, the perpetrator of this attack on one of Broadway's most beloved performers was apprehended backstage. The villain was none other than Trish Gibson, one of the lead producers and the wife of Harold Gibson, her partner in producing, but not in crime.

To tell you the truth, one need not see Miss Drake almost killed because, to turn a phrase, she's in a killer show and giving a performance to die for, so be sure to see this remarkable performance and show.

But Dawna Drake's performance isn't the only delicious performance in this show. You will be delighted by the excellent work of Clarrisa Roman. She's simply amazing, not only when singing but in her delivery of her many barbed comments. Without giving anything away, all I can say is you'll find yourself never wanting her to give you a cup of coffee. The audience loved her, as did I.

I wish I could say the same for Marshall Ward, who plays Drake's love interest. For someone who has third billing, the poor man had hardly any part at all, and for some strange reason the few lines he has were often delivered with his back to the audience. I wonder what Allison Duprey, the director of this show was thinking. Other than that, Mr. Duprey's direction was razor sharp as ever.

As for the creative staff, all I can say is BRAVO! Elina Fay's costumes, while not always consistent for Miss Drake, are overall spectacular, especially the ones in the second act. Fiona Williams' lighting is sensitive, handsome, and supportive, but then her work is always top notch. As for Jen's set designs, while the first act is mostly just good solid work, his transition into the ballroom at the end of Act One is stunning. A friend, who I spoke to during intermission, told me that the transition was reminiscent of the sets for the original "My Fair Lady". Well, all I can say is if you are going to steal (and I use the term lightly) then steal from the best. Bravo Jens!

And last but certainly not least is a newcomer named Kevin Travis, the show's choreographer. While he hasn't been given a lot of stage time, he has used it remarkably well. Who knew Dawna Drake could dance? What a revelation that was and what a pleasure to see her partnered by the handsome and supportive Romain Rodgers. I look forward to seeing more of Mr. Travis' work, hopefully in the near future.

There's not enough space in this review to mention all the other actors and their delicious performances. All I can say is go see them. They are simply terrific!

Folks, this is one of those rare, stunning shows that will have you leaving the theatre with a smile on your face and a copious collection of outstanding memories to treasure for a long, long time. I'm mad about the gal and I'm mad about the show!

About the Author

Ray Klausen has had a wide and varied background ranging from being a top television and theatre set designer for over 400 productions, including nine Broadway shows and ten Academy Awards shows, resulting in his winning three Emmy Awards. He has worked with such celebrities as: Michael Jackson, Prince, Cher, Streisand, Madonna and Elvis, to name a few.

His first book, *Behind the Scenes: From Hollywood to Broadway,* is a remarkable history of the television and theatre world from the late1970's to the early 21st century.

Duplicity, Ray's first Inspector Willis murder mystery, was published in 2022.

Coming soon:

New Inspector Willis adventures:

"Deep Duplicity"

and

"Duplicity, Care to Die?"